MW01491814

PRAISE FOR FOLK TALES FOR
HEALTH & WELLBEING

'A real treasure of insightful stories with lessons that have inspired me to be a better person.'

Marie Parkinson, yoga teacher and author

'A wonderful retelling of traditional folk stories from around the world that will, I am sure, resonate and inform.'

Shakyapada Roberts, the York Buddhist Centre

'A charming selection of wonder-filled, bite-sized legends from all over the world, retold in Bushnell's inimitable style … The kind of book the world needs right now.'

Eleanor Conlon and Martin Vaux, podcasters and authors of The Three Ravens Folk Tales

Folk Tales
for
Health &
Wellbeing

ADAM
BUSHNELL

Illustrated by Bea Baranowska

First published 2025

The History Press
97 St George's Place, Cheltenham,
Gloucestershire, GL50 3QB
www.thehistorypress.co.uk

Typesetting and origination by The History Press.
Printed and bound in Great Britain by TJ Books Limited, Padstow, Cornwall.

MIX
Paper | Supporting
responsible forestry
FSC® C013056

Trees for Life

Contents

Acknowledgements

I'd like to thank Nicola Guy and all at The History Press for their continued support.

My thanks also go to Shakyapada Roberts from the Buddhist Centre in York for her help with the Buddhist sources.

Special thanks to my editors Harry and Dee.

Introduction

I've worked in education for more than twenty-five years as a visiting author and as a teacher in both private and state education across the UK and internationally. My degree was in philosophical studies and I've trained under several faith advisors on mindfulness and meditation for over thirty years. But I'm also a storyteller. We all are.

We thrive on stories in all of their forms, whether news articles, stories in the pub or experiences at work that we share at the dinner table. We communicate through story. We express our inner selves in the retelling of the story. It holds great power.

We are story animals and we always have been. When our ancestors first developed the ability to communicate, share experiences and pass on knowledge, we became storytellers. Long before writing was invented, early humans relied on oral traditions to transmit knowledge, culture and history. Stories were passed down from generation to generation, serving as a way to teach survival skills, convey moral lessons and explain natural phenomena.

Some of the earliest evidence of storytelling comes from cave paintings and other forms of symbolic art created by early humans. These images, found in places like Lascaux in

France and Altamira in Spain, date back tens of thousands of years. The paintings often depict scenes of hunting, animals and human figures, suggesting that early humans were telling stories through visual means, possibly as a way to record important events or share communal myths.

In Will Storr's book *The Science of Storytelling*, he describes just how much stories feature in our day-to-day lives, from reading up on people's life experiences on social media, to listening to podcasts on your way to work to unwinding with a Friday night film. These shared experiences show just how often the art of story features in our everyday lives, giving us something to relate and connect to.

Stories help us make sense of complex realities. By organising information into narratives, we can better understand cause and effect, human motivations and the broader context of events. Stories give meaning to facts and experiences. The stories we tell about ourselves and our lives shape our identities. Personal narratives help us understand who we are, where we've come from and what our future might look like.

Stories provide a way to process and make sense of our emotions, which is why I wanted to write this book. These stories have been selected as they can help us to explore our feelings about subjects such as loneliness, anger, fear, jealousy and loss. They might help us to ask questions about what it means to be wise, generous, kind or loving. The tales explore death and immortality and what it means to live a 'good' life. Some of the tales are therapeutic and can help us cope with difficult situations too.

We are naturally driven to find meaning in our lives and these tales are a way to construct that meaning.

We must never underestimate the power of stories.

Bruno Bettelheim, the Austrian psychologist, explains how fairy tales educate, support and liberate the emotions of children in his book *The Uses of Enchantment*. I wholly agree.

Introduction

Fairy tales are powerful developmental tools for children and adults alike.

In this collection of my favourite teaching tales from around the world I have included ones that contain tragedy, comedy and hope.

There will be both familiar and unfamiliar tales here. There are familiar characters like Anansi the trickster spider and Icarus, who doesn't listen to the advice of his father. We have three tales about Jack, of beanstalk fame. But we also have perhaps unfamiliar characters like Judge Cai Fu, An Tiêm the wise and Sun Xiyao the herbalist. We have stories from Buddhism, Christianity, Judaism, Islam and Taoism. Some I have read and retold from books, others I have heard from other storytellers and have reimagined them here. But lots I have collected when visiting countries such as China, Vietnam, Greece, Malawi, UAE, Qatar and more. I have interpreted them in my own way.

The aim of these tales is to empower you to live better lives free from anxiety and stress as much as is possible. Breathe deeply, relax, smile often and be grateful as often as you can.

Enjoy!

Adam Bushnell
September 2024

I

The Angels in the Tower

When we 'fly too close to the sun' we do something especially ambitious and daring. But this can ultimately lead to our undoing or downfall. This expression is an allusion to the mythical character Icarus. Here we see what can happen when we become overly ambitious when trying to reach for something that is unattainable without help or advice from others.

On the island of Crete, King Minos' face contorted with fury, his eyes narrowing into fiery slits. He clenched his fists as veins throbbed at his temples. His breath came in ragged bursts, each exhale a growl. The room seemed to vibrate with his escalating rage.

'Dead?' he snarled.

'MY MINOTAUR IS DEAD?'

The king's voice shook the stone walls of his palace.

The trembling messenger regretted being the bearer of such news. Minos was not a king to take bad news lightly.

'And this is the work of that King Aegeus' son?' Minos' furious scowl twisted into a predatory grin, like a crocodile savouring the moment before devouring its prey.

'I know just what to do. Bring me Daedalus. He will create something truly terrible, something that will show the Greeks no one dares to defy me!'

Daedalus was the king's inventor. It was he who had created the maze for the Minotaur, an intricate labyrinth of tunnels. The designer and engineer had been happy to create the maze. It would save lives, after all. It would contain a creature that feasted on humans. But Daedalus was now horrified when he learned of Minos' demand this time. The king wanted a flying machine to rain fire upon villages, towns and cities, a harbinger of death and destruction. Daedalus shuddered at the thought of thousands dying. He could not, would not, build such a monstrous device.

But how could anyone refuse King Minos?

Daedalus began to pace. He and his son Icarus had been kidnapped over a year ago, snatched from their peaceful lives in Athens, where they crafted ingenious inventions. Minos had heard of their talents and brought them to Crete, where they became prisoners on the island in all but name.

Daedalus gazed out from the window of their tower, the highest point on their prison home. From there, he could see the sprawling palace below, the endless sea, and, on clear days, the distant coastline of Greece.

A pigeon landed on the windowsill, interrupting his thoughts, and left behind a single grey feather. If only Daedalus and Icarus could be as free as birds, soaring over the water to return home. He picked up the feather, turning it in this way and that. He smiled.

He would build a flying machine, but not the one Minos envisioned.

Icarus returned home from fishing, looking dejected.

'Not a single bite today, Dad.'

'Perfect! Hand me your fishing line,' Daedalus exclaimed.

Icarus stared at the mess in his father's hands, a concoction of feathers and wax.

'What are you making?' asked Icarus.

'Making our escape!' Daedalus beamed, holding up the proto-type; a row of feathers bound with candle wax.

'What's it meant to be?'

'Wings!'

'What for?'

'We're going to fly off this wretched island!'

Icarus' face became wrinkled and soon smoothed to a wide grin.

'Collect every feather you can find, every piece of fishing line, twine, rope and candle wax. But do it secretly! No one must know.'

Icarus and his father skulked around the island collecting the items needed. Nobody paid them any notice. The pair were often collecting seemingly useless objects and turning them into incredible things as demanded by the king.

In two days, the wings were complete.

King Minos was convinced that Daedalus was working on his war machine. He sat on his throne scowling at his loss but relishing in the revenge he would take.

Daedalus used melted wax to attach the first pair of wings to Icarus' back, then his own. They looked at each other, the wings folded against their backs.

Daedalus' wings were a marvel. They gleamed in the sunlight, each feather perfectly aligned to catch the wind. The delicate structure, both fragile and resilient, promised freedom.

'My greatest invention,' Daedalus grinned.

Icarus smiled nervously.

'We'll leap from the window. Pull the ropes to open the wings, catch the wind and glide to mainland Greece. Don't fly too low, or the sea spray will dampen the wings. Don't fly too high, or the sun will melt the wax. Do you understand?'

Icarus wasn't listening. He stared out the window, imagining the leap into nothingness. What if the wings didn't work? What if they fell apart? But he trusted his father.

'I'm ready, Dad.'

'You go first, son. I'll be right behind you.'

Icarus closed his eyes, took a deep breath, and stepped off the ledge. He opened his eyes and pulled the ropes. The wings stretched open, and Icarus soared into the sky.

Daedalus followed and they glided past the palace and over the sea. He could only imagine the look on King Minos' face when he discovered their escape. Daedalus smiled.

Icarus was euphoric, feeling the rush of wind beneath his wings. He soared with exhilaration, the wind rushing past his face as he climbed higher. He laughed, feeling the sun's warmth on his back and the sheer joy of flight. He looped and dived, revelling in the freedom, his wings slicing through the air. Higher and higher he climbed, basking in the sun's warmth.

'Remember what I said!' Daedalus called. 'Don't—'

But Icarus wasn't listening. He looped and twirled, flying closer to the sun. He felt something wet trickle down his back and thought it was sweat. But it wasn't sweat; it was wax.

The feathers began to loosen and float away. Icarus' triumph turned to terror as his wings disintegrated, wax melting in the sun's heat. Feathers scattered, and he plummeted, flailing helplessly. The wind roared past, drowning his screams. His body struck the sea with a devastating splash, swallowed by the unforgiving waves, leaving only ripples where he once soared.

Daedalus watched helplessly as his son fell. He knew it was too late. Icarus was dead.

Heartbroken, Daedalus didn't go to mainland Greece but flew on to Sicily, where he lived in mourning, never inventing again.

When Daedalus finally died, he was reunited with Icarus in the Underworld, and there, in the realm of shadows, they found peace together.

Folk tales are stories that usually have people or animals as their main characters, but myths are stories told to explain the world around us. This story is a myth that would have been more of a folk tale of the time. The word 'myth' comes from the Greek 'mythos', which meant story. Stories teach us many things, in this case why listening to wise and trusted people is essential for our own wellbeing.

2

The Birth and Early Life of Siddhartha

The Jataka tales are a large body of literature in the Buddhist tradition that recount the previous lives of the Buddha in both human and animal form. This particular story from India, often known as 'Siddhartha and the Swan', is not found in the Jataka tales, yet it shares a similar purpose: to convey moral lessons and demonstrate the Buddha's compassion, wisdom and virtue.

More than 2,500 years ago, in the lush kingdom of Kapilavastu, nestled on the borders of what is now Nepal, reigned the noble Sakya king, Sudhodhana. His realm was a tapestry of rolling hills and serene valleys, yet within his splendid palace there lurked a sadness. Despite the lavishness that surrounded them, King Sudhodhana and his beloved queen, Maya, were childless. The absence of an heir weighed heavily upon them.

One night, under the vast canopy of stars, Queen Maya drifted into a deep and restful sleep. As she slumbered, a dream of unparalleled strangeness and beauty unfolded before her eyes. She envisioned a celestial baby elephant, pure and white as freshly fallen snow, descending gracefully from the heavens and entering her body. In that moment, the air filled with the sweet strains of divine music, trees and bushes burst into vibrant bloom, and lotuses spread their petals across the serene lakes. The entire world seemed to rejoice, enveloped in an aura of profound celebration.

The following morning, Queen Maya recounted her extraordinary dream to the king. The palace buzzed with anticipation as Brahmin priests were summoned to interpret the vision. With solemn faces and reverent tones, they foretold that the queen would soon bear a son, a child destined to become either a mighty king or a revered sage. True to their prophecy, a few months later, the queen gave birth to a radiant baby boy. The joyous parents named him Siddhartha, meaning 'one who achieves his aim'.

From his earliest days, Siddhartha was enveloped in the lap of luxury. The palace was a paradise for children, adorned with every conceivable comfort and delight. The young prince's days were spent amidst the sprawling gardens, learning and playing with his cousins and friends. His closest friends were his cousin Ananda, his loyal squire Chandak and his beloved horse Kantak.

Siddhartha grew into a child of exceptional kindness and gentleness, endearing himself to everyone in the palace, save for one. His other cousin, Devadatta, harboured a deep-seated jealousy and resentment towards Siddhartha. Devadatta loathed his cousin's compassion and the universal love he commanded. Devadatta seized every opportunity to provoke and antagonise the young prince, seeking to undermine him at every turn.

One spring morning, Siddhartha wandered to the river that meandered through the palace gardens. There, he paused, captivated by a group of swans gliding gracefully on the shimmering water. Their pristine white feathers were touched with liquid gold by the bright sunlight, creating a vision of ethereal beauty. Siddhartha gasped in awe as his heart swelled with admiration.

As Siddhartha sat by the riverbank, lost in the tranquillity of the scene, an arrow suddenly sliced through the air with a sinister whistle. It struck the largest and most majestic of the swans, causing the bird to cry out in agony and thrash its wings in desperate fear. Siddhartha rushed into the river to rescue the wounded creature. The swan, unable to swim or fly due to its broken wing, flailed helplessly.

With gentle hands and soothing words, Siddhartha cradled the swan, calming it as he carried it back to the riverbank. There, he carefully removed the arrow and fashioned a splint from a nearby stick, using a strip torn from his own clothing to bind the wing. His compassion and tenderness transformed the chaos into a scene of quiet healing.

Soon, Devadatta arrived, breathless and furious, searching for his arrow. He had seen the swans and, in a cruel twist of envy, decided to use them as targets for his archery practice. 'The swan is mine!' he declared, his voice sharp with arrogance. 'I shot it down and it is mine! Get off it!'

Siddhartha replied calmly, 'I saved it, cousin. It is mine to care for now.'

'Fine,' Devadatta sneered, his eyes narrowing. 'We'll take it to our guru and he will tell you that the swan is *mine* because I shot it with *my* arrow.'

The two children carried the injured swan to their guru, who listened to Devadatta's tale with a discerning ear. Then he turned to Siddhartha, his gaze soft but probing. 'What do you have to say, Siddhartha?'

Siddhartha took a deep breath and then said with a voice steady and filled with conviction, 'The swan was simply swimming gracefully upon the river. It was minding its own business and doing no harm. Then Devadatta shot it. If he has the swan then he will harm it again. I have healed it and I will care for it until it is well enough to fly again.'

The guru smiled warmly, his eyes twinkling with wisdom. 'The swan is now Siddhartha's. Siddhartha saved its life. He healed it and will care for it.

'Devadatta sought to harm and destroy. Ownership of a living being belongs to the one who loves and protects it. Thus, the swan shall be with Siddhartha.'

Devadatta's face twisted with rage. He stormed off, vowing vengeance. But Siddhartha remained serene, his heart light with the knowledge that he had done right by the swan. He tended to the bird until its wing healed completely, then released it back into the river, watching it rejoin its flock with a sense of profound peace.

As Siddhartha grew, the prophecy of his birth unfurled. He became a great sage, among the greatest the world has ever known. Siddhartha Gautama, through his compassion, wisdom and quest for enlightenment, became the Buddha, guiding countless souls on the path to inner peace and liberation.

Siddhartha's actions highlight the importance of compassion and kindness towards all living beings. He instinctively chose to protect the swan, emphasising the value of life. The story teaches that life is precious and should be preserved.

The story also foreshadows the teachings of the Buddha, who later emphasised non-violence (Ahimsa) and compassion to all living things as central tenets of his teachings.

3

King of the Beasts

Many monarchies have deep historical roots. They have often evolved over centuries, becoming intertwined with national identity and cultural traditions. They can provide a sense of stability and continuity. Different countries have different reasons for maintaining their monarchies, reflecting their unique historical, cultural and political contexts. However, in this story, a king's authority is challenged by the unlikeliest of opponents ...

A long time ago, before the world had been reborn to make way for the humans, the king of all the animals on earth was the lion. He was a majestic and magnificent beast. Each morning his golden mane shone with a thousand shades of bright light. He had a roar that could shake the heavens and this roar would summon all the animals of the earth to come and bow to him as their rightful king.

However, one morning, a rabbit was sleeping soundly on a soft bed of lush, green grass. The rabbit felt so cosy and comfortable that it didn't want to go and bow to the lion. He really didn't see the point other than massaging the ego of the already well esteemed lion. Anyway, who would miss a little rabbit? The lion would be too busy basking in his own magnificence to notice if the rabbit was not there.

The sun was warm on its fur and the gentle breeze carried the rich scent of blooming flowers. The rabbit soon fell into the deepest, sweetest sleep.

After some time, the rabbit awoke to a slight chill in the air. It had become dark. The rabbit sleepily blinked its eyes open to find it was not night time. But rather a large shadow loomed over the terrified rabbit. It was the lion who towered over the rabbit, casting a cold shadow of fury. The lion's eyes blazed like molten gold and his mane shimmered like a halo of fire.

'You lazy, ungrateful, disrespectful little creature!' roared the lion. 'How dare you sleep when you are meant to bow to me?'

The voice of the lion was thunder and his eyes were focused with fury. The rabbit's heart pounded like a drum. What should the rabbit say? What should the rabbit do?

Very politely, it said, 'I'm sorry Your Majesty but this morning when I got up to go to make my way to bow to you, I came to a river and in it was a huge demon. I was afraid and ran up here a few minutes ago to hide in this grass.'

The lion's eyes narrowed.

He eventually asked, 'Did the demon hurt you?'

The rabbit quickly shook its head.

'No,' answered the rabbit, trembling. 'It didn't hurt me but yelled as I went by. It asked me where I was going.'

The lion sat down as the rabbit continued.

'I said that I was on my way to bow to the king of all the earth. It asked who that was and I said that it was you, lion.

'It laughed, lion. It laughed at you.'

The lion stood up and roared so loudly that the clouds shook and the trees trembled.

The rabbit went on, 'The demon then said that it would be the new king. I was to tell you to go down to the river and it would challenge you there. It would be waiting beneath the water for you.'

The lion roared again.

'There isn't anything on this earth or anywhere else that can defeat me!'

'Should I take you to the river?' asked the rabbit timidly.

The lion swished his tail and shook his mane. The rabbit took this for an affirmative and led the lion to the river, which glistened like a ribbon of liquid silver under the blazing sun. The water was so clear that it mirrored the surroundings perfectly.

'Where is it?' growled the lion. 'I'll fish that demon out of the water and tear it to shreds!'

'Right there,' pointed the rabbit. 'Look.'

The lion looked into the river and saw his own reflection in the water. His hair all bristled up and his tail lashed from side to side. The reflection seemed to the lion a formidable opponent. The rabbit began dancing up and down on the bank, yelled, 'There it is! There it is!'

The lion flew into a great rage. He let out a deafening roar, and with a mighty leap, he jumped into the water to fight his perceived rival. The water churned and frothed as the lion thrashed about, his roars turning into desperate gurgles. In his fury and confusion, he didn't realise he was fighting his own reflection. The more he struggled, the deeper he sank, until finally, the great king of beasts drowned himself in the depths of the stream.

The rabbit watched as the waters stilled and the ripples faded away. He sighed in relief and hopped back to his soft bed of grass, where he could once again enjoy the warmth of the sun and the sweetness of the day. He soon fell into a deep sleep.

Perhaps the moral of this Tibetan folk tale is that the mighty lion was no match for his own pride. But it also raises the question of how the rabbit could be so morally disengaged as to watch the lion drown then sleep so peacefully? Which then could raise the question of why people do bad things without feeling guilty about them. Psychologists have suggested that feeling guilt is good for you. Guilt leads to shame but this gives us the capacity to confront, learn from and heal from it. Those who cannot do this have either suppressed their awareness or lack it altogether, leading them to distract themselves, dismiss their feelings, and live in denial of their true selves. Guilt can help us to become self-aware and can help us to grow.

4

Jack and the Fish

Jack features in many folk tales. He's usually a foolish character but wins in the end through charm, wit and trickery. However, in this particular tale we see how an act of kindness can have a far-reaching effect on the protagonist's good fortune. Good deeds lead to good things!

Jack was a lazy man. The trouble was he just didn't like working. When he got home one day after losing yet another job his wife said to him, 'Oh Jack. I'm sick of this! We can't live on the money you bring home. The fishing trade is booming. Why don't you go and try to get a job on one of the boats?'

'Oh, but I don't like fish!' moaned Jack. 'They're all wriggly and slimy and they haven't got any eyelids, they look at you all the time. Blurgh! No, I don't like fish!'

'Go and be a fisherman or we'll starve!' his wife shouted.

Jack went out of the front door and trudged down the road towards the harbour. Once there, he soon got a job on board a boat and was out to sea that same day.

But Jack made a useless fisherman; he threw his rod into the water as soon as he had caught a fish, claiming that he didn't like the way it looked at him. So, the captain of the boat gave Jack a net to see if he'd get on any better with that. In no time at all Jack had caught a huge ball of mackerel. He hauled the net on to the deck of the boat and opened it up.

The mackerel danced and flitted around the deck and there in middle of these jumping fish was a fine salmon. This fish didn't move, it lay perfectly still and seemed to be looking up at Jack.

'I can't kill this animal. It's beautiful!' thought Jack to himself.

He then picked up the salmon, made sure no one was looking, leant over the side of the boat and let the fish go. It disappeared into the water but not before it made a 'plop' sound.

'Are you throwing away my haul!' bellowed the captain. 'That's it, I've had enough Jack! You're sacked! Here's a couple of pennies, that's all you've been worth to me today.'

Once back at the harbour, Jack trudged slowly along the road home. As soon as he got through the door his wife looked at him and said, 'Well I know that look. You've lost another job again, haven't you? Here, take my wedding ring. Head down to the market and sell it.'

'I can't sell your wedding ring!' exclaimed Jack. 'It took me, you know, days to save up for it.'

'Go and sell the ring or we'll starve!' shouted his wife.

Jack took the ring and trudged once more down the road. As he walked, he wondered who on earth could help him. There surely must be someone who would understand his plight.

As Jack thought this he bumped into a tall man.

'Oh I'm terribly sorry, I didn't see you!' said Jack.

'That's quite all right, Jack,' the man smiled.

This tall man was dressed in a fine black suit, he was wearing a top hat, carried a cane and had a dark goatee beard.

'How do you know my name?' asked Jack.

The man flashed a dazzling smile and his green eyes burned brighter.

The man spoke in smooth and silky tones. 'I know a lot about you. I know you are having money trouble. Perhaps I can be of assistance. Perhaps you would like to borrow my cow?'

The man clicked his fingers, and there standing in the middle of the road was a fine Jersey cow with bulging udders that needed milking right away.

'Wow!' blurted Jack. 'I'd love to loan your cow! That's a healthy-looking animal that. But what do you want from me?'

'Oh, nothing much,' smiled the man. 'You can borrow my cow for, let's say, one year. At the end of the year, I'll come back and ask you three questions. If you get the questions right, you can keep the cow. If you get the questions wrong … then I'll take your soul!'

'That sounds like an excellent idea,' laughed Jack. 'You've got a deal.'

Jack shook hands with the man and took the cow by her collar up the road. When Jack looked back the man had disappeared. Jack shrugged and skipped up the lane, leading the cow home.

'Blimey Jack!' said his wife. 'You've done well there! That cow for my wedding ring!'

'Even better!' laughed Jack. 'Here's your wedding ring back. I met a man who has loaned us this cow for a year. At the end of the year he'll ask me three questions. If I get them right we keep the cow! Good eh?'

'What if you get them wrong?' asked his wife suspiciously.

'Then he takes my soul.'

'What!?' screamed his wife. 'I don't mean to be rude Jack, but you're an idiot. That man was the devil. There's no way you'll get three questions right. You've sold your soul … for a cow!'

'Then I shall go to the *library*!' said Jack proudly. 'I shall read books and make myself clever!'

Jack went off to the library every day. He read book after book after book. It was the hardest he had ever worked in his life.

His wife, she milked that cow every day and turned their house into a café. There she sold milk, butter, cheese and yoghurt.

Once the year was over, Jack came home from the library and said, 'Well wife. Time is up. Today is the day the devil comes to ask his three questions.'

'Oh Jack!' she sobbed and rushed upstairs.

Jack stood behind the counter of the café. He looked around, it was practically deserted. Just one stranger sat in a corner. He had a hood pulled over his head and had only a glass of water in front of him.

Suddenly, the devil appeared with a flash in front of Jack.

'Hello Jack!' smiled the devil. 'Are you ready for your three questions?'

'Yes,' answered Jack. 'Yes I am ready.'

The stranger in the corner of the café leapt to his feet and bellowed, 'THAT is your first question!'

'What?' spluttered the devil. 'What's going on here Jack?'

'I don't know what's going on, I swear!' answered Jack.

'THAT is your second question!' boomed the stranger.

'Who is that man Jack?' demanded the devil.

'I don't know, I've never seen him before!' answered Jack.

'And THAT is your third question!' roared the stranger. 'You've had your three questions and you've had your three answers, now be gone with you devil!'

The devil's face flashed a scarlet colour, his eyes glowed emerald green, he stamped his foot on the ground and disappeared into a puff of dark grey smoke.

Jack turned to the stranger and asked, 'Who are you?'

The stranger lowered his hood as he moved toward Jack. His skin had a silvery sheen to it, his eyes were perfectly round, he had no eyelids and on his neck were three lines on one side and three lines on the other.

'I am the King of the Fishes,' the stranger said. 'One year ago you saved my life. Now I have returned to save yours … use it wisely Jack.'

With that the stranger turned and walked out of the café.

Jack and his wife lived happy lives. But if you were to go into that café you would see a black mark on the ground. It doesn't matter how many times that black mark gets scrubbed or how many times that black mark gets rubbed, nobody can remove the black mark where the devil disappeared in a puff of smoke so long ago.

In a Halloween episode of The Simpsons, *Homer signs away his soul to the devil in exchange for a doughnut. When Homer eats the last bite the devil reappears to claim the soul. But Homer's wife, Marge, eventually stops the devil by pointing out that Homer pledged his soul to her years ago on their wedding day, therefore the contract is invalid. The devil concedes and Marge has saved her husband.*

Deals with the devil in folk tales are often a metaphor for entering into a contract with an evil person. This could be in business but it can also be applied to the relationships we have. Spending time with the right person is essential for our wellbeing.

The Unicorn

In Celtic myths and legends, the unicorn is a symbol of purity, innocence and healing. Stories of unicorns date back further than the Ancient Greeks. Aristotle, the Greek philosopher, wrote about what unicorns looked like and described them as 'one-horned donkeys' and he believed that they originated in India. Whatever the origin, the unicorn is the official animal of Scotland and was chosen by King Robert III in the 1300s. It is now on the Scottish Royal Coat of Arms and remains a symbol of nobility and power. This story shows the unicorn's power to cure any poison, even when it comes from the devil himself.

Long ago in Scotland all the animals lived in perfect harmony. The cat and the dog were the best of friends. The fox and the mouse shared stories every night. The deer and the wolf played games together. They lived like a huge happy family.

Scotland itself was the most beautiful home the animals could ever wish for. Wild flowers bloomed and the trees blossomed. Huge mountains glowed purple and sandy beaches glittered golden.

The animals would gather together by a huge loch at sunrise and at sunset to drink and talk. In the day they would watch the sun rise together and in the evening they would watch the sun set, and see the lush green landscape glow red, orange and yellow before turning blue and purple. The white light of the moon would guide them home and each would sleep blissfully looking forward to their next day.

But … something had sneaked into Scotland at night. It had left its home of Eden. It was the serpent. The serpent was a creature of evil. It loved nothing better than to spoil beautiful things. It loved nothing better than to watch things burn, rot and wither. It watched with jealousy and rage as it saw the animals living together so peacefully.

So, the serpent slithered and slimed its way towards the loch once all of the animals had left and had fallen asleep. It stared at its own reflection in the water. It hated what it saw. It hated itself even more than it hated others. It dipped its tail into the loch and ripples distorted its features. Poison dripped from its tail into the loch. The poison spread across the surface, then mixed with the pure water. It poured all of its hate and loathing out and the loch turned black. The serpent then slithered off to cause more mischief elsewhere.

The next morning the animals gathered around the loch. The stench rising in clouds of green mist was revolting. The animals became scared. They knew that if they drank from the lake then they would die. They ran and hid.

The day turned to night. The night turned to day. The animals howled and moaned. They roared and groaned. Their thirst was too much to bear. Their suffering could be heard all over Scotland. One of the animals was unlike the others. This animal drank from a loch on top of a tall mountain in the Highlands of the north. It had remained hidden from all, but when it heard the howling and moaning of suffering, it came down from the mountain. It came down to help. This was the unicorn. It was a glowing white horse with a horn that twisted and turned from its forehead.

The unicorn trotted slowly in the light of the moon to the loch. It sang a song so beautiful that all the other animals stopped their crying and shouting to listen. They all walked, padded and crept towards the poisoned loch. They saw the unicorn glowing in the white moonlight.

Once all of the animals were gathered, the unicorn stopped singing and slowly lowered its horn into the water. Gently, the white horn broke the surface of the black water and was submerged from its tip to its base. The lake began to clear. The water turned from a murky black to crystal clear. The unicorn raised its head away from the water and took a few steps backwards.

The animals all eagerly stepped towards the lake and drank. They drank and drank until their bellies were bursting. They all smiled at each other and then turned to the unicorn. But the creature had gone.

It had trotted away into the Highlands of Scotland, where it still lives today, hidden from view by most. But some lucky ones have seen it. Perhaps you are one of those fortunate folks.

The unicorn waits. For if evil were ever to return, then the unicorn will always be there as the guardian to protect us all.

After hearing the story above, Queen Elizabeth I of England used to drink from a cup made from a unicorn horn as she believed that it would protect her from poisoning. The cup was actually made from a narwhal horn as, along with dragons, centaurs and mermaids, the unicorn is a mythical creature, and does not exist, despite what we might wish for. But evil could be considered real. Evil could manifest itself in the form of an addiction, theft or neglect. When people act in a way we perceive as 'evil' then we cannot rely on unicorns to protect us. Instead, we should spend time with trusted friends, stay positive and keep away from negative people. These three rules for life can be our unicorn.

6

The Lonely Lord

Even those who seem to have everything long for something else. Often this is something that cannot be bought. In the case of the protagonist in this tale, it is the company of another. Vivek Murthy, the US Surgeon General, said in 2023, 'Loneliness and isolation represent profound threats to our health and well-being.'

You don't have to be wealthy to enjoy the company of a lifelong partner. But partners only become lifelong if there is mutual respect and appreciation. The following tale tells of a misguided desire for something that cannot be bought: love.

In a grand castle nestled within vast lands, a wealthy lord with many riches and possessions suffered from a profound loneliness. His heart was untouched by the warmth of companionship and he yearned for a partner to share his life.

One day, as the lord rode his fine stallion through his vast estate, he passed a modest farmer's house. Oblivious to the boundaries of propriety, the lord trotted into the farmer's garden to admire the flowers. There, he noticed the farmer's daughter, a young and beautiful girl, tending to the blooms.

Approaching her with a charming smile, the lord said, 'Good day, my dear. I couldn't help but wonder if you might consider becoming my wife.'

The farmer's daughter, unimpressed, retorted, 'What? I'm not marrying you. You're old, and you're ugly. No way!'

With that, she retreated into her home, leaving the lord in a state of indignation.

Enraged by the unfamiliar rejection, the lord marched to the front of the farmer's house, demanding an explanation. He hammered at the door, which was answered by the father of the girl.

'Erm, yes, my lord? Can I help you?' asked the poor farmer.

'Indeed, you can!' boomed the lord. 'I just asked your daughter to marry me ... and she said no! Is it not a great honour for me to propose to your daughter?'

'It is sir,' replied the poor farmer.

'And would she not be rich beyond her wildest dreams?' demanded the rich lord.

'She would sir,' answered the poor farmer.

'And is it not right that she should agree to marry me then, eh?' the rich lord said in a menacing tone.

'Erm, well I suppose it is sir.'

'Right then!' bellowed the rich lord. 'You have just promised me your daughter's hand in marriage!'

'But—' began the poor farmer.

'No "buts" man! A promise is a promise,' said the rich lord, shaking his hands in the air and walking back to his stallion. 'I will set the wedding for one week's time at the church. And your daughter had better be there!'

The poor farmer, who felt that he was compelled to comply with the lord's wishes, reluctantly agreed to the proposed marriage.

A week later, an extravagant wedding had been planned. The church was decorated and a sprawling marquee was put up for the reception.

The lord's impatience grew as he waited inside the church. Where was his bride to be? She was late!

Unable to tolerate the delay any longer, the lord sent a messenger to the farmer's house to demand what he believed was rightfully promised to him. The farmer's daughter would be his wife and would make him happy. That was the deal. The farmer had agreed after all, hadn't he?

The messenger had arrived at the farmer's house. He knocked at the door and when the farmer's daughter answered the messenger said, 'The rich lord says that he wants what's been promised to him.'

'Oh, I see,' replied the poor farmer's daughter, thinking quickly. 'He's talking about a horse! There's a female horse he's been wanting from us. You know – a mare for his stallion. She's down round the back of the garden, help yourself!'

The quick-witted and resourceful girl watched as the messenger hurriedly led the horse to the church, where it was tethered outside.

'I've done it!' the messenger said as he re-entered the church. 'She's outside.'

'Right then,' beamed the rich lord. 'Take her to my castle and lead her into my mother's bedroom.'

'What? Why?' asked the messenger.

'Just do it,' answered the rich lord gruffly.

'What if she struggles when I'm getting her up the stairs?' asked the messenger, rather bemused.

'Then get some friends to help you. Now go!' snapped the rich lord.

So the messenger untied the horse and led her to the rich lord's castle. With some help he got the horse up the stairs and into the bedroom. He then rushed back to the church and said, 'I've done it! She's in your mother's bedroom.'

'Excellent,' grinned the rich lord. 'Now dress her in fine silks and exquisite velvet. Give her some jewellery and some make-up too.'

The messenger stood with a wrinkled brow.

'You heard me, now do it!' snapped the lord.

Following the lord's whims, the messenger then adorned the horse in fine silks, velvet, make-up and jewellery.

'I've done it, she's wearing a fine gown and she's all made up,' the messenger said.

'Now bring her to me … I wish to marry her!' leered the lord.

'You want to what?' gabbled the messenger.

'You heard me now do it!'

'OK then,' shrugged the messenger as he sped back to the castle. He then led the horse down the stairs, out the doors and along the road to the church.

When the messenger got there, he flung open the church doors. The congregation erupted in laughter upon seeing the horse in a wedding gown.

The horse stared at the lord.

The lord stared at the horse.

The horse let out a loud neigh and bolted from the church as fast as she could. Outside the church, the lord's stallion, captivated by the sight of the horse in the wedding dress, fell in love instantly. The two equines galloped away to live happy lives together.

As for the rich lord?

He was left to grumble in his castle surrounded by his riches yet forever denied the love and happiness he sought but never truly understood.

This cautionary tale, originally from Norway, is intended to both entertain and serve as a warning. We can accumulate wealth, possessions and status but do these things really make us happy? It is human connection that essentially provides us with happiness. Each of us can begin our happiness journey by strengthening and developing the connections and healthy relationships that we already have.

7

Rabbit in the Moon

Self-sacrifice is the theme of this next tale. When we perform random acts of kindness, such as letting someone out of a junction or paying for the coffee for the person behind you in a queue, we improve our own mental health. Studies have shown that by showing others kindness we reduce our own stress, improve our emotional wellbeing and it even benefits our physical health.

In a forest far away, there lived four friends: an otter, a monkey, an elephant and a rabbit. Each animal was quite different. The otter used to keep her food to herself, never sharing with anyone. The monkey used to love playing tricks on his friends. The elephant was so greedy that he used to gulp down all the fresh water from the spring without letting anyone else have a drink. But the rabbit was different. She was kind, loving and sharing. She used to tell the others stories before they went to sleep. Her stories were full of characters that always shared, never played tricks on people and were certainly not greedy. The more she told these stories, the more the others began to change. Soon the otter shared her food with her friends. She discovered that if you share with others, then others share with you.

The monkey stopped playing tricks on his friends. He discovered that people like you much more when you're nice to them rather than playing tricks on them. The elephant stopped being so greedy. He discovered that by slowing down when he ate and drank, he enjoyed his meals much more.

One night, after the rabbit had told a story about helping others in need of help, she said, 'I've got an idea.'

The others looked her and saw she was smiling.

'We have everything that we need in our forest. Let's give some food and drink to the people that live in the village beyond. I've heard people begging there. I've heard hungry children crying.'

The four friends agreed that this was a most excellent idea. So, the next day the otter caught a great pile of fish. The monkey collected huge bunches of bananas. The elephant sucked up fresh spring water until his trunk was bursting. The rabbit collected and wove together long, strong reeds from the river to make plates and cups.

They then left the food and drink outside of the village and hid among the trees.

Some children were playing nearby, and when they eventually spotted the food and drink, they were delighted. Those children shared what they had found with everyone.

Each day the four friends would collect more food and drink, and each day they left the feast out for the people from the village. These kind acts did not go unnoticed. God had been watching.

So, one day, God came down to earth to meet these four remarkable friends. God came disguised as an old beggar man wearing tattered clothes and rags, bent right over on a gnarled stick. God came walking through the forest moaning and groaning, pretending to be dying of thirst and starvation. The beggar sat down on a large rock and moaned some more.

The otter noticed and leapt from the river to present fish to the beggar, who smiled and built a small fire to cook the fish.

The monkey then came swinging through the trees and gave the beggar a banana for dessert. Then the elephant came pounding through the forest and squirted some fresh water into the beggar's mouth.

Finally came the rabbit. But poor rabbit had nothing to offer the beggar. She looked here and there, and finally hopped on to the beggar's lap.

'I have nothing to offer you ... apart from myself. Take a knife and cut off my fur. You can use it to keep you warm.'

'But you will die!' exclaimed the beggar.

'So will you if you don't find warm clothes. The forest may be warm now but it gets very cold at night. Do it ... have my fur.'

There was a blinding flash of light.

The beggar disappeared and all that could be seen was white light throughout the forest. The four friends heard a loud voice inside of their heads saying, 'I have seen such kindness from you all. I thank you. I am so very proud of you. But you rabbit ... you are the kindest of all. You would have given up your own life to help another. You put others' needs before your own. You are a shining example to all.'

With that, God lifted up the rabbit into the sky and placed her on the moon. There the image of the rabbit remains to this day. Whenever the moon is full the rabbit shines her light down upon us all to remind us how we should always treat others as we would want to be treated.

This might be an extreme example of how we can help others, yet sacrificing our own gains and needs for others can have a profoundly positive effect on our own sense of fulfilment and overall happiness. An altruistic approach to life is seen to benefit us in four ways according to mentalhealth.org.uk. These are:

Helping others feels good as there is evidence to suggest that there are physiological effects on the brain that are linked with happiness.

It creates a sense of wellbeing and reduces isolation.

Helping others, especially those less fortunate than yourself, can help put things into perspective and make you feel more positive about your own life.

The benefits of helping others can last long after the act itself, both for you and them.

8

The Tiger, the Brahmin and the Dog

A Brahmin is a priest in the Hindu religion. This story is from Indian folklore and tells of how a dog helps a Brahmin escape from being eaten by a tiger. I have changed the original jackal character to a dog, and have also merged another folk tale of how dogs came to live with humans, as both folk tales seemed to fit together so well.

In a lush forest, where sunlight filtered through the thick canopy of trees and birds sang melodiously, there resided a Brahmin. This Brahmin was enjoying the warmth and sounds of the forest but after a while he knew he needed to return to the temple.

As the Brahmin was walked through the forest, he stumbled upon a tiger that had been trapped in a cage.

'Let me out,' the tiger said with a toothy smile.

'If I let you out then you'll eat me,' the Brahmin replied.

'No, I won't,' the tiger said with an even larger smile. 'Let me out.'

'Do you promise you won't eat me?'

The tiger nodded. The smile was huge now.

'I promise. Now let me out.'

The Brahmin nodded then unlocked the cage and opened the door. The tiger leapt out and began to stretch.

'Ah! That's better. I was so cramped in there. I was in there for so long that I'm starving. So now, I'm going to eat you.'

'But you promised you would not,' the Brahmin said with a shake of his head.

The tiger shrugged and prepared to pounce. Just then a dog came walking along. The dog looked at the man and the tiger.

'Morning!' smiled the dog.

'Ah and dessert has just shown up too!' the tiger leered at the dog.

'Run!' the Brahmin shouted. 'Or you'll be eaten.'

'Hungry, are you?' the dog asked the tiger.

'Indeed I am! After being stuck in that cage for so long I now have quite the appetite.'

'So, you were in the cage?' the dog asked the Brahmin.

'No, the tiger was in the cage.'

'You were both in the cage?' the dog then asked.

'No, just the tiger.'

'Where were you then if the tiger was in the cage?'

Suddenly, the tiger roared, 'I was *inside* the cage! He was *outside* of the cage!'

The dog smiled and said, 'I don't think I quite understand. Can you show me?'

The tiger snarled and climbed back inside the cage.

'I was in the cage like this,' the tiger began but before it could finish the dog barked at the Brahmin, 'Lock the door!'

The Brahmin locked the door, thanked the dog and set off for the temple. The dog followed the Brahmin several paces behind. When the Brahmin arrived at the temple he went inside to pray. The dog meanwhile decided to explore.

There were jars of powdered paint that the Brahmin used to touch up the colourful paintings on the walls of the temple.

The dog was looking for somewhere to sleep out of the bright afternoon sun, so it jumped up into one of the jars. The dog settled down on the soft powdered paint and began to sleep.

A little later, feeling refreshed, the dog stretched, then leapt from the jar and strolled back into the forest.

Just then, an elephant saw the dog and gasped.

'You're blue!'

The dog looked at its fur, and sure enough it had been dyed blue by the powdered paint.

'Blue is the colour of God!' the elephant went on. 'Have you come to walk among us simple creatures?'

The dog wagged its tail.

'Yes,' it grinned with mischief on its mind. 'I have come to see what life is like for mortal creatures.'

The elephant let out a loud cry of delight. Soon other animals from the forest came to see what all the fuss was about. The elephant instructed each one to gather gifts for the dog. Monkeys gathered fruit, birds collected seeds, deer stripped bark and offered this as a drinking bowl, and tree toads collected moss to make a soft bed. The animals waved large leaves to fan the dog. They sang songs of adulation for the blue celestial canine.

After a while the tiger came to the gathering.

'What's going on here?' asked the tiger.

The elephant gladly explained that it was she that had found the blue dog. The tiger's eyes narrowed as she carefully examined the dog.

Above the forest, dark clouds had gathered. Soon large raindrops fell and dripped through the tree canopy. They dripped down and soaked the animals beneath. Including the dog. The animals gasped as they saw the blue paint wash away in the rain.

'I knew it!' snarled the tiger. 'You've been tricked! Let's get that dog!'

The dog raced away as the animals chased after it. The dog burst into the temple and begged the Brahmin to help.

'Please hide me!'

The Brahmin gave the dog sanctuary. The animals would not enter the temple without invitation. They waited outside for a while but eventually gave up and went back into the forest.

'I can never go back into the forest,' the dog said sadly to the Brahmin. 'I will never be welcome there again.'

The dog hung its head low. The Brahmin smiled.

'Then you can stay with me in my home.'

The dog's tail wagged at great speed.

'Really?'

'We shall be a companion for each other.'

This is how the Brahmin came to share his home with the dog.

In the Hindu holy book, Bhagavad Gita, *it is written that all living things should be treated equally. As such, dogs, cows, birds and monkeys are frequently found in temples in India.*

In this story, the dog saved the Brahmin from being eaten by the tiger. But is this why the Brahmin repaid the favour by saving the dog? Do we only do kind things because we think that we might be repaid in the future? According to the American Psychiatric Association, new research suggests that performing acts of kindness may help reduce symptoms of depression and anxiety by boosting your mood and reducing stress.

9

The Sage of Medicine

This Taoist folk tale from China tells of a healer who shows true wisdom by not seeking personal gain or glory, but instead uses his knowledge and skills for the greater good.

During the Sui dynasty, there lived a remarkable herbalist named Sun Xiyao, a man whose very name whispered of the ancient secrets of the earth. From the tender age of 6, Xiyao was drawn to the healing arts as naturally as a river flows to the sea. By the age of 12, his knowledge of herbs was already as deep as the roots of the ancient trees that lined the mountains, his skill in diagnosing illness surpassing that of the most seasoned physicians. His touch was a balm to the sick, his prescriptions a cure for ailments that left others baffled.

Sun Xiyao dedicated his life to the arts of longevity and the mysteries of life itself. He brewed and tested all manner of herbs until he had mastered them all.

One day, as he wandered along the banks of a tranquil river, gathering herbs with the diligence of a bee collecting nectar, he noticed a flash of green in the tall grass. Drawing closer, he saw a small, emerald-hued snake lying limp, its life force ebbing away like the last rays of the setting sun. Xiyao knelt beside the creature. His hands, steady as a sculptor's, opened his medicine case. He smeared a fragrant ointment on the snake's wounded body, the cool balm soothing the creature's pain. Then, with the wisdom of the ancients guiding him, Xiyao crushed herbs into a paste and gently fed it to the snake. Moments passed in breathless anticipation. The snake lifted its head in a gesture that seemed almost grateful. Slowly, it slithered away, disappearing into the underbrush, leaving Xiyao with the quiet satisfaction of a healer who has restored life.

Days later, while Xiyao was once again gathering herbs by the same river, an old man appeared. His robe, woven from threads of red and gold, shimmered in the sunlight, and beside him walked a child dressed in green, his steps light and quick like the breeze. The old man approached Xiyao, bowing deeply, his eyes reflecting the wisdom of ages.

'I am forever in your debt,' the old man said, his voice as smooth as polished jade. 'You saved my grandson's life. Come, my child, and thank the man who gave you back your life.'

The child stepped forward and bowed to Xiyao. As their eyes met, realisation dawned upon Xiyao: the child was the very snake he had saved.

'We are snake spirits,' the old man continued, 'the guardians of this river. May I invite you to our humble dwelling for a meal in your honour?'

Sun Xiyao, though surprised, nodded his consent. The old man took his hand, and with a gentle tug, led him into the river. As Xiyao's feet touched the cool, flowing water, the world around him shimmered and transformed. The river opened up like a doorway into another realm, revealing a grand mansion beneath the surface, where the air was thick with the scent of the finest seafood, arranged in a feast that dazzled the senses.

But Xiyao bowed respectfully to his host and said, 'I have abstained from eating living beings. Please do not be offended if I partake only of seaweed and river grass.'

The old man's eyes softened with understanding. 'You are wise beyond measure. Name a gift you would like to have, and if it is within my power, I shall give it to you.'

Sun Xiyao replied, 'You need not give me any gift. As a healer, it is my duty to save all living things.'

The old man sighed, a sound like the wind rustling through the leaves. 'Even so, I must express my gratitude. For years, I have watched you gather herbs along this river, your dedication unmatched. I will give you a catalogue of the herbs that grow along these banks, along with a guide on their uses.'

Xiyao's eyes lit up with quiet joy. 'I will honour your gift and will use this knowledge for the good of all living things,' he promised.

Returning home, Sun Xiyao immersed himself in the study of the herbal catalogue. Day after day, he pored over the pages, his mind absorbing the wisdom of the river spirits. Soon, his reputation as the Medicine Sage spread far and wide, his name spoken with reverence in every corner of the land. Eventually, even the emperor himself heard tales of Xiyao's unparalleled skill.

The Sui emperor sent for Sun Xiyao, inviting him to serve as the court physician. But Xiyao declined. To his closest students, he confided, 'The emperor is an ambitious man, his heart set on the elixir of immortality. But such desires lead only to ruin. I fear his dynasty will not last long.'

Indeed, Xiyao's foresight was true. The Sui dynasty, weighed down by harsh laws and heavy taxation, crumbled after a mere twenty-nine years, swept away like leaves in an autumn storm. The Tang dynasty rose in its place, ushering in an era of prosperity under the wise rule of Emperor Taizong.

Taizong heard of Sun Xiyao's legendary wisdom. He sent emissaries to invite the sage to his court, but Xiyao, ever modest, refused to accept any official post. 'Please tell His Majesty that I cannot accept, but I would be honoured to advise him on matters of medicine.'

Eventually, Taizong's persistence paid off and Sun Xiyao was brought before the emperor. The moment Taizong laid eyes on him, he exclaimed, 'I have heard that there are sages who never grow old, but this is the first time I have seen one! How have you remained so youthful in appearance?'

Sun Xiyao smiled. 'People often seek longevity for the wrong reasons. Some fear death while others are ensnared by vanity. I am but a simple man who dispenses herbs to heal illness. There is no elixir of immortality, only the quiet peace that comes from living a life in harmony with nature. My herbs can cure the body, but they cannot grant eternal life.'

The emperor listened, his brow furrowed in thought. 'I now understand what it means to cultivate longevity,' he said slowly. 'Though I would like to devote my life to spirituality, I know that my duty lies with my people. Their needs must come first.'

Sun Xiyao bowed deeply. 'Your Majesty is wise. It is your duty to rule, just as it is mine to heal. I will stay and advise you as long as my knowledge can be of use.'

Sun Xiyao returned to his humble abode, where he spent his final years documenting his vast knowledge of medicinal herbs. He passed away peacefully at the age of 90, his life a testament to the harmony between man and nature. As he breathed his last, a mist filled his room, wrapping his body in a shroud of tranquillity. It was said that in that moment, two snakes, intertwined like the yin and yang, appeared to carry his spirit away to the heavens.

This story suggests that the pursuit of immortality is misguided. Sun Xiyao highlights the futility of the human obsession with immortality. The quest for eternal life is not only unattainable but also distracts from the more important aspects of living a virtuous and meaningful life. Human lives are impermanent. What truly endures is the legacy of one's good deeds and the knowledge passed on to future generations.

10

Silver Hair

Here we have a cautionary tale better known as 'Goldilocks and the Three Bears'. However, in this retelling I've written it in the style of Eleanor Mure's version from 1831. This is the first recorded version and we see Goldilocks as a silver-haired old woman who breaks into the house of Cecil Lodge (Mure's family home). The bears discover her, then try to burn and drown the old woman. They eventually 'chuck her aloft on St Paul's church-yard steeple'. This retelling takes those elements and tells the tale as it was originally intended rather than how we know the story today.

Winter wounded with wind. The old woman pulled her cloak ever more tightly as she trudged over the white-blanketed landscape. Her milky eyes narrowed as she saw the house. It was dark but her silver hair sparkled in the moon just as the snow sparkled back. She pulled up her hood, covered her moon-like locks and stepped silently forward.

Peering in through the window, she saw an empty house.

The old woman moved swiftly and stealthily like a cat. She tried the front door and smiled. A thin, joyless thing. She slipped inside and allowed her eyes to adjust to the deeper dark.

Her movements were all with purpose. She pulled out a sack and began to feed the cavernous thing. Ornaments, jewellery, cutlery, all of it went in. Only the downstairs was raided. Upstairs, snores could be heard and that would be too risky.

When the sack was impossibly full, she heaved it on to her back. Old she may have been but her will fed her strength. She slipped out of the door and heard a creak on the top of the stairs behind her.

A burly voice was shouting down at her.

She slammed the door and was away. But the sack made it difficult to escape to shelter. A bare-chested barrel of a man was bounding towards her. She cursed. Dropped the sack and fled.

The old woman made it to the trees and crouched low. The man searched for a matter of minutes, then collected the sack and returned to his home.

Lights were lit and doors were locked securely. The old woman lowered her hood and narrowed her eyes. Cursing again, she set off into the woods.

Houses in this part of the world were few and far between, but as the morning mists began to swirl around the trees, she saw another. This house was sat in the centre of the woods. The owners were up early. Smoke came from the chimney and the sound of men talking could be heard.

She gripped a tree and stared.

The front door opened and three men appeared. They carried fishing rods and backpacks. They closed the door, without locking it, and then set off into the woods in the opposite direction from the old woman.

She moved her cheek muscles in the way one might smile. As the sun shone through the branches above, she pulled up her hood. She was into the house in a flash. A second sack was pulled from her cloak and she looked around.

The kitchen was filled with fishing lines, rods, hooks, bait.

There was a large chopping board that displayed fish guts like a speciality of the house. Knives, hooks, cleavers were strewn about.

She peered into the larder. On one shelf rotten fish alive with maggots filled the small room with a powerful stench.

There was another shelf with fish covered in salt. She knew it was to keep the meat fresher for longer but she couldn't bear the taste.

She grabbed a handful of smoked fish from a third shelf and stuffed the lot into her mouth. She chewed noisily and bits of fish fell to the floor.

She hadn't realised how hungry she was until she began to eat.

When her belly was silent, she began her search for anything valuable.

The search was long and fruitless. The house was a mess and everything in it was worthless.

In frustration she kicked at the only three chairs in the living room. A small rocking chair fell as she did so and broke as soon as it made contact with the floor. The broken pieces did not look out of place among the rest of the chaos. She searched every room downstairs, then made her way up. Every stair creaked and groaned. There were only two rooms on the upper floor. A bathroom and a bedroom. The bathroom was coated in dust and filth. There was certainly nothing of value in there.

She cursed once more and walked into the bedroom. Three beds of different sizes lay in a line and nothing more. The old woman pulled down her hood and threw her sack on to the ground in frustration.

She sat on the smallest of the beds and sighed.

She knew she was too old for this lifestyle. She knew she was not as successful as she once was. Previously she was able to live like a queen for a month after only one night's work. But now ...

She sighed again and lay down.

She only closed her eyes for what she thought was a moment but they snapped open as she heard the front door do the same. The three brothers were talking and laughing, but then stopped instantly. Their voices became low and hushed. She leapt from the bed and landed on her feet. The traitorous floorboards squeaked noisily.

She looked around the room wildly and fell to the floor. She squeezed herself under the bed as the stairs creaked and groaned under the weight of three pairs of feet. The three brothers stepped into the bedroom. She peered from under the bed and saw that each carried a large knife.

The first brother threw his bed over like it weighed nothing.

The second brother did the same.

She closed her eyes.

The third brother threw his bed and they surrounded her.

She opened her eyes and looked up. Their hands were upon her as viciously as their looks. They grabbed and lifted her. The third brother opened the window and laughed.

The others joined in. A deep, throaty, horrible sound that a large wild animal might make. They carried her to the window and threw her out.

She landed with a terrible squelching sound. Her bright blood ran and stained her silver hair.

The three brothers walked calmly down the stairs and began to chop up their new bait to catch more fish.

It would seem that this gruesome story doesn't do much for your health and wellbeing at first glance. However, the key message of the story is not just to warn us not to enter other people's homes uninvited, but rather we should not intrude on people's privacy. Respecting people's privacy is important in order to build trust. Every individual values their own privacy. To intrude upon this is like trespassing into someone's home. It is like eating their porridge or like sleeping in their beds. We all have a right to privacy.

II

Judge Cai Fu

This Taoist folk tale from China is a teaching tale. Taoists often told these stories in the imperial courts of the Sui, Tang and Song dynasties. They were to show that both body and mind are only developed through training and simple living. They were also intended to demonstrate that the wisest people devoted themselves to honour and justice. Justice is very much the theme of this particular tale ...

During the Tang dynasty, there was one a man named Cai Fu who was revered as the 'Incorruptible Judge'. His name struck fear into the hearts of wrongdoers and commanded the deepest respect from the virtuous. His was a justice as cold and clear as the mountain streams, untouched by the warmth of mercy. His wisdom extended far beyond the realm of the living.

By day, Cai Fu presided over the provincial court, his presence looming like a shadow over those who dared to cross the lines of righteousness. But as the sun dipped below the horizon and darkness cloaked the world, his duties took a more spectral turn. Cai Fu was no ordinary magistrate. His judgments were feared not only in the world of the living but also in the shadowy, echoing halls of the afterlife, where no soul could hide from his gaze. For at night, Cai Fu donned the mantle of a judge in the court of the underworld. There he meted out justice to the souls of the dead.

One fateful year, the governor of the province where Cai Fu resided issued a decree: hunting was forbidden on Taoist festival days, days sacred to the balance of life and death. Yet, there was a hunter, a man of rugged sinew and iron will, who thought himself above the governor's edict. He saw the wild deer in the forest as his by right, not as creatures to be spared by the whims of a far-off ruler.

With a sharp twang of his bow, the hunter loosed an arrow and a deer fell, its lifeblood staining the earth in a crimson pool. His victory however was short-lived. As he approached his fallen prey, soldiers seized him, their hands cold and unyielding as iron shackles, and they dragged him before Cai Fu.

The courtroom was silent, the air thick with the scent of incense and tension. Cai Fu sat on his high bench, his eyes like two dark pools that reflected nothing. His voice, when it came, was as steady as the passing seasons.

'You are guilty of violating the prohibition against hunting,' Cai Fu intoned, each word falling like a hammer on an anvil. 'You shall be punished.'

The hunter's heart pounded in his chest like a drum, his bravado melting under the judge's piercing gaze. But Cai Fu, with a slight, knowing smile, offered him a choice: 'I will let you choose your punishment. You can take fifty lashes from the whip now, or you may go to my court in the underworld to receive your sentence there.'

The hunter, who had faced wild beasts and the harsh elements without flinching, now thought himself clever. The underworld? How could a man be punished in a realm he had not yet entered? Only a fool would choose the whip. Aloud, he said, 'Your Honour, I choose to receive justice in the underworld.'

Cai Fu's expression remained inscrutable as he nodded and waved the man away. Released, the hunter felt a surge of triumph. As he walked out of the courtroom, he chuckled to himself, a grin spreading across his face like a crack in stone. 'Today, I have outsmarted the judge,' he boasted to his companions. 'Let's see what he can do to me in the underworld.'

That night, the hunter's pride swelled within him, even as the moon cast ghostly shadows across his room. But as he drifted into sleep, smug with his supposed victory, a sudden gust of wind tore through his chamber, cold as death's touch. The hunter bolted upright, his eyes wide in the darkness. Before him stood two figures, monstrous and nightmarish, their forms twisting like smoke in the moonlight. One held a club that gleamed with an otherworldly menace, while the other carried a scroll, its ancient parchment crackling as if alive.

'You are hereby summoned to the court of the dead,' one of the monsters declared, its voice a growl from the depths of the abyss. The words sent a shiver through the hunter's soul. He barely had time to protest before he was bound in chains as cold as the grave and dragged from his bed. The world around him spun and darkened, and when he could see again, he found himself in a vast hall, its ceiling lost in shadows, its walls echoing with the cries of the condemned.

There, upon a bench carved from stone as black as a starless night, sat Cai Fu, his presence more imposing and dreadful than ever. The hunter's knees buckled, and he collapsed, his earlier bravado shattered like glass.

Cai Fu's voice cut through the air, sharp and unforgiving. 'This morning, you chose to be judged in the realm of the dead,' he said, his eyes boring into the hunter's very soul. 'I hereby pronounce your sentence. Because you have killed on a day dedicated to honouring life, your own lifespan will be reduced. The years you have taken from the deer will be deducted from your own life.'

The hunter's blood ran cold. He begged, pleaded for mercy, but Cai Fu was unmoved, as unyielding as the mountains. 'I gave you the choice of punishment this morning,' the judge said. 'You chose to be punished here in the underworld, thinking you could escape justice. Justice is dispensed in the realms of both the living and the dead. Had you chosen punishment in the realm of the living, you would have recovered from your injuries in a matter of weeks. But by trying to escape justice, you have forfeited years of your life.'

When the hunter awoke the next morning, drenched in a cold sweat, he was a changed man. The underworld trial haunted his thoughts, like a shadow that he could never escape. He avoided the forest, steered clear of anything that might tempt fate. He examined bridges with caution before crossing, avoided arguments with the fervour of a man who knew death's breath was ever near. But the passage of time dulled his fear, and soon, the memory of that terrible night began to fade. The years passed, and the hunter's mind turned back to his old ways. 'Perhaps it was just a dream,' he thought, dismissing Cai Fu's judgment as nothing more than a spectre of his imagination.

Five years later, on an ordinary day, the hunter walked into a shop to buy provisions for another hunting trip. The air was thick with the scent of spices and dried herbs, the shop bustling with the mundane activity of daily life. But as the hunter reached for a bag of grain, a deep, foreboding rumble echoed through the building. Without warning, the ceiling above him gave way and came crashing down. The hunter, and only the hunter, was killed instantly.

In the end, the hunter learned that there was no escape from Cai Fu's justice, whether in the world of the living or the domain of the dead. The years of life he had so carelessly taken from the deer had indeed been deducted from his own, just as the Incorruptible Judge had decreed. Justice, like death, was inevitable, a force that neither wit nor will could evade.

This tale is meant to show that justice is inescapable. The choices we make and the actions we take carry consequences that cannot be avoided. Trying to outsmart justice or avoid responsibility only leads to harsher and more inevitable repercussions. This tale serves as a reminder that moral integrity and accountability are essential, as justice will ultimately be served, regardless of time or place.

12

The Golem

The classic narrative of 'The Golem' tells of how Rabbi Judah Loew of Prague (known as the Maharal, 1525–1609) creates a golem to defend the Jewish community from antisemitic attacks. According to one version, the Jewish community, under the rule of Holy Roman Emperor Rudolf II, faced violent persecution and false accusations of using Christian blood in their rituals. To safeguard his people, Rabbi Loew crafted the Golem from clay gathered from the banks of the Vltava river. In this tale I have amalgamated lots of versions into this more generic one …

Long ago, in the heart of Prague, there ruled an emperor whose insatiable lust for gold was limitless. His castle was filled with golden objects of every sort: vases, plates, bowls, lamps, candlesticks, coins, rings, necklaces, mirrors, shields, swords and more. The northern wing of the castle was built to house his collection, which gleamed and glimmered. The emperor would sit for hours and hours simply staring at the glittering golden treasure store.

The emperor's desire for gold was matched only by his hunger for magic, which knew no bounds. He was convinced that magic was everywhere and became utterly obsessed with the dream of transmuting base metals into gold. He called forth a legion of magicians and sorcerers to his court. They would fill not only the northern wing but the whole castle with gold. The walls themselves would become made of pure gold. But as each attempt ended in failure, the emperor's fury was relentless. He punished their incompetence by severing their hands and cast them aside like broken tools.

The emperor's advisors, desperate to find their ruler's approval, and to quieten the fury within in order to save their hands, or their heads, whispered of ancient secrets hidden within the sacred texts of the Jewish people. Perhaps, they suggested, these mystical scriptures held the elusive key to alchemical success.

The emperor soon latched on to this idea and became obsessed with nothing else. The Jewish people had the secret. He just knew it!

As twilight fell upon the city, the rabbi watched with growing dread the swelling crowds gathering at the gates, their numbers increasing night by night. Rumours, like wildfire, spread that the Jews harboured hidden treasures. Fear gnawed at the rabbi's soul, for he knew the danger this pointless envy posed to his people.

But what he could do to protect his people? They were peaceful and even if they were called to fight, they would be no match for the emperor's army. Something had to be done. But what?

Driven by desperation on a moonless night, the rabbi made his way to the riverbank. Amidst the murky waters and moss-covered stones, he sculpted a figure from the clay using a simple wooden spoon. With trembling hands, he inscribed ancient Hebrew letters upon its forehead and placed a shem, which was a clay tablet inscribed with God's secret name, within its mouth. In that instant, the Golem stirred to life, a guardian born from mud and mysticism, an embodiment of divine protection.

The Golem stood at an imposing 8ft tall, its massive frame casting an ominous shadow. Its eyes burned with an orange, flickering light, reminiscent of smouldering embers in a darkened forge. The glow pulsed rhythmically, illuminating the night with a haunting, otherworldly radiance that seemed to pierce through the very soul of anyone who dared to meet its gaze. The rabbi knew that the Golem was ready to defend the Jewish people at any cost. It would give its life in return for their safety. It would be the guardian of the gate. Surely the emperor's mob would run in terror and leave them alone forever.

But the Rabbi didn't want to be this confrontational. He hid the Golem away in his home. It had to stoop considerably to get inside, but once safely stored, the rabbi sought an audience at the opulent palace. There, before the emperor's sceptical gaze, he engaged in a lengthy discussion. The rabbit talked of peace between the Jewish community and the emperor's subjects. The rabbi spoke eloquently and patiently, reasonably and light-heartedly, but to no avail.

So, the rabbi spoke of a protector of unparalleled might that could be summoned to guard the Jews. This story captivated the ruler.

'How could such a creature be made?' the emperor asked with a suspicious look.

'With this!' smiled the rabbi.

He handed over a simple spoon.

The emperor turned it this way and that and cast it to one side.

'Have this man removed! He is a charlatan and a liar!'

The rabbi was thrown out of the castle and walked back to his people. There he opened the door of his home and guided the Golem to the gate. There it stood guard. Ready and waiting. A vigilant sentinel of the ghetto, unyielding.

One fateful night, an enraged mob surged forward, their intent bent on destruction. The Golem's eyes blazed with an otherworldly light as it unleashed its wrath. As the mob pressed closer, the Golem's fury grew. They pushed at the gates and yelled at the Jewish people. The Golem hit the gates, causing them to reverberate, and sent the crowd back slightly. But then they surged forward again. So, the Golem hit out again. This went on a few times and each strike of the gates made the Golem grow larger, its strength more fearsome. Eventually, it shattered the ghetto's barriers and the people screamed in terror. They ran away but the Golem was not finished with them. It wrought havoc upon the city and made its way up to the emperor's castle. It hammered at the walls, which crumbled at once under the assault.

The rabbi looked on in horror. What had he done? The Golem had to be stopped!

The Golem then lifted the entire castle from its formations. It shook the whole building so vigorously that all inside were killed instantly, including the emperor. Then the Golem placed the castle on its head, like a crown; a sign of its victory.

In desperation, the rabbi scaled the immense Golem and retrieved the shem, that sacred clay tablet, from its mouth. The creature fell silent at once, returning to its lifeless state of clay.

As years turned to centuries, stories of the Golem wove themselves into the very fabric of Prague. Some believed the Golem's shattered remnants were repurposed to rebuild the city. Others whispered that the Golem lay dormant beneath the hill upon which the palace stood. A few clung to the eerie notion that the Golem had escaped, lurking in the shadows, awaiting the day it would be summoned back to life.

Or perhaps, as time marched on, all that remains of the Golem is the stories.

Many Jews view the Golem as a symbol of resilience and the enduring spirit of a people who have faced centuries of persecution. Perhaps the Golem's story can also be seen as a meditation on the nature of power itself. The Golem is immensely powerful but also dangerous. This duality reflects the broader human experience with power, where the same forces that can protect and build can also destroy and corrupt.

13

An Tiêm and the Watermelon Seeds

This folk tale is famous through all of Vietnam. I heard the story when visiting both Hanoi and Ho Chi Minh City, where it was performed as a water puppet show. It is sometimes known as 'The Watermelon Prince' and is about how the things we do can affect our future even if these deeds go way back into the past ...

An Tiêm was an orphan. He was only 7 years old. What would he do? He was all alone. He lived near a harbour and a kindly sailor found the boy wandering the streets. After learning his fate, the sailor decided to hire the boy as a helper on a merchant ship that traded silk and spices from India for medicine from Vietnam. All on board the ship quickly came to like An Tiêm for his hard work and eagerness to help, especially the captain.

In those ancient days, Vietnam was under the benevolent reign of King Hung Vuong the Third. The king was adored by his subjects for his kindness and generosity.

Upon their return, the merchant ship's captain decided to pay his respects to the king. He also decided to take An Tiêm with him. When the pair paid their respects, the king asked about An Tiêm. When the king heard the boy's story, in his wisdom and compassion, he immediately chose to adopt An Tiêm and raised him with love and care. The boy grew into a wise and skilful young man, earning the admiration of the entire kingdom, especially the king himself.

The king was blessed with a single daughter named Oanh. As the years went by, the king saw An Tiêm and Oanh become good friends. He saw that this relationship had soon turned to love for each other. With the intelligence and potential of An Tiêm, the king arranged for him to marry his daughter, believing that An Tiêm was destined to rule the land after his passing. Their wedding was a grand celebration filled with joy, and they were gifted a beautiful castle to call a home of their own. An Tiêm and Oanh loved each other deeply and their union was blessed by the heavens. Soon they were graced with two wonderful children.

However, the king's favour towards An Tiêm sparked jealousy among some of his courtiers. The boy had been given the role of foreign minister, overseeing the trade from overseas, which was a much-coveted position. The boy did well and soon became very rich but he was not motivated by money. He merely wanted the best for the kingdom and he knew that foreign trade would achieve this.

Over time, this envy of the courtiers festered into hatred. Desperate to remove An Tiêm, they concocted malicious rumours, accusing him of plotting to usurp the throne. These lies spread like wildfire, and despite their falsehood, they reached the king's ears. Although heartbroken, King Hung Vuong felt compelled to protect his kingdom from potential betrayal and called for An Tiêm to confront him about the rumours.

'I am not ungrateful Your Majesty,' the boy began. 'I have worked hard but I'm certain my good fortune is down to deeds I performed in former lives. The seeds planted in a former life are the fruits reaped in this life now.'

'So, you believe that your good deeds from your former life led me to take you into the palace?' asked the king.

'I do!'

'Therefore, if I was to exile you to a desolate island with your wife and children then you would all survive and come back to me … all because of the seeds from your former life?'

The boy nodded.

The king stroked his chin.

'Very well, I banish you, Oanh and your children to the island of Sa Chau. We shall see if you are right about these seeds of former lives and fruits of fortune!'

Stripped of their former luxuries, An Tiêm with Oanh worked tirelessly to survive. They built their own shelter, fished for food and made life bearable for their children. They could not find any fruit on the island though, and they longed to cultivate their own fruit and vegetables.

One scorching morning, while hunting, An Tiêm noticed birds pecking at strange black seeds. Curiosity piqued, he gathered a handful and brought them home. With hope in his heart, he scattered the seeds around their hut.

Months passed, and tender shoots sprouted from the earth, creeping along the ground. Under the broad leaves, fruits began to form, growing until they were the size of a head. The smooth-skinned fruits had a delightful fragrance, and when cut open, revealed a sweet, crimson flesh. An Tiêm, Oanh and the children tasted the red miraculous fruit and it was the most delicious thing they had ever eaten.

A flock of cranes flew overhead. An Tiêm knew these to be birds of good luck, so he chopped up some of the red melon and fed it to the cranes. The birds devoured the melon and, enchanted by its sweetness, cried 'dưa hấu', which meant 'watermelon' and so the fruit was named. The cranes then flew away with the tasty watermelon still in their beaks.

The family harvested the watermelons, storing enough to sustain them. They saved the seeds to plant more around their home. Over time, their watermelon crops flourished, providing ample food.

There was an unexpected visit from a passing trade ship to the island. Their ship's sails were torn and they anchored nearby. When the boats arrived on shore, An Tiêm and Oanh rushed to help the sailors. With the sails mended, the couple offered slices of melon to the sailors.

'These are delicious!' exclaimed one.

'Can we have more?' another asked.

'We will trade with you!' the captain added.

So, in exchange for the melons, An Tiêm and Oanh received beans, sugar, salt and rye.

'If you return on your way home, then we can trade more melons with you.'

The sailors agreed heartly and did indeed return in four months.

This time An Tiêm and Oanh traded for various seeds and spices but also for tools and building materials.

The word of the watermelon soon spread, and every month a ship stopped by to trade every manner of thing for the tasty watermelons.

The sweet red melon became in great demand, so An Tiêm and Oanh planted more and more black seeds and harvested hundreds and hundreds of melons. The watermelons became so high in demand that the couple were eventually able to build a grand house, wear fine clothes, rear livestock and hire some workers from the mainland, who lived in a small village they built on the island.,

Back in the palace, King Hung Vuong deeply missed An Tiêm and his daughter, unaware of their fate. An Tiêm, sitting by the beach, often gazed towards his former home, reflecting on the twists of fate.

Four years had gone by, until one day a trade ship captain arrived at the king's palace with some slices of the watermelons as a gift. When the king tasted the fruit, he was amazed.

'I must go to the land where these are grown! I must see these incredible fruits and how they are grown!'

King Hung Vuong was taken on board the captain's ship and taken to the island. He saw the village and marvelled at the wonderful house built by the harvester of the watermelon. An Tiêm and Oanh came to greet the new visitor. When the king saw his daughter and son-in-law he leaped with joy, knowing his beloved family was alive. He was filled with pride and admiration for An Tiêm and Oanh's ingenuity.

'My boy,' the king beamed. 'You said that the seeds of your past deeds determine the fruits of our future and I truly believe you!

'I'm so sorry and humbled by you and my daughter. Please return to the mainland with me.'

King Hung Vuong then bowed to the boy and offered him the crown. An Tiêm accepted, and from that day forward, he ruled Vietnam with the same wisdom and compassion as his adoptive father, bringing prosperity and peace to the land. But the first thing he did as king was to plant watermelons throughout the kingdom.

'Your deeds are our monuments' is an Ancient Egyptian proverb meaning that what we do has far-reaching consequences into the future. It emphasises the idea that the actions and good deeds we perform during our lives are the lasting legacies we leave behind, far more enduring than physical monuments or memorials. It reflects the universal value placed on virtuous actions and their lasting impact on the world. Whether you believe in previous incarnations or not doesn't necessarily matter. What does matter is acting virtuously now. But, who knows, it might help our future selves.

14

The King's Ears

I have heard and read variations of this Ancient Greek tale from lots of places, including Ethiopia, Malawi and Hawaii. The main message always remains the same though: we all have things about our appearance that we don't like. Perhaps another lesson we can learn from the story, though, is to always choose diplomacy when a powerful god asks you what you think of his music.

In Greece, there was a traveller who went from place to place seeing the sights and meeting new people. One day, he arrived at a town he had never visited before. He spent the day walking the streets until he arrived at the market place. There, he saw the king of that land, King Midas, riding past on a magnificent Arabian stallion. King Midas was dressed in luxurious robes and on top of his head he wore a turban. Nobody else was wearing one so the traveller guessed that King Midas wasn't wearing the turban as part of his religion. Maybe it was a fashion accessory.

The traveller went to a tavern, ordered a drink and said to the barman, 'Excuse me, but why does your king wear that turban?'

'Don't mention the turban!' the barman hissed. 'King Midas is very sensitive about it! He never takes it off and if anyone questions him about it … he chops their head off! Don't mention the turban … *ever!*'

This made the traveller even more curious and eventually he got a job in King Midas' palace sweeping the floors. One day, the traveller was sweeping a long corridor when he heard strange singing coming from along the way. The traveller walked a little further, stopped and listened.

The traveller realised that the singing was coming from behind a closed door in front of him. He pressed his ear to the door and listened again.

The traveller then peered through the keyhole and saw that it was King Midas sat in a bath and singing.

King Midas was washing his hair as he sung, and the traveller saw that the king was not wearing his turban. The traveller also saw *why* King Midas wore the turban. The king did not have a pair of ears that you would usually see on a human. The king had what appeared to be donkey's ears.

'My goodness!' exclaimed the traveller to himself. 'King Midas has got donkey's ears!'

He rushed out of the palace and into the tavern.

'Barman!' said the traveller. 'Give me a drink quickly. I've had quite a shock! I know why your king wears that turban. You see King Midas –'

'Shh!' screeched the barman. 'Don't mention the turban! I've told you before! I don't want to know why he wears it! I want to keep my head on!'

'B – But I've got to tell someone!' moaned the traveller.

He felt that this secret would burst out of him if he didn't share it.

'Well,' said the barman, 'why don't you go down to the riverbank, dig a hole and shout the secret into the hole. It'll make you feel better.'

The traveller rushed to the riverbank and dug a hole with his hands like a dog. When it was about the size of a bucket, the traveller put his head inside the hole and shouted, 'KING MIDAS HAS GOT DONKEY'S EARS!'

It was such a relief to shout out the secret that he did it again, 'KING MIDAS HAS GOT DONKEY'S EARS!'

After he had shouted out the secret many times, the traveller went back to the palace to finish his work.

Eventually, the traveller decided to move on to another town to carry on exploring.

Many years passed. It was King Midas' sixtieth birthday coming up and he wanted to throw a party in his palace. Everyone in the town was to be invited. King Midas sent for his musicians and said, 'Musicians, I want you to compose a piece of music about how wonderful I am. I want you to perform this at my birthday party to everyone.'

'Of course, Your Majesty,' said the musicians, bowing low.

But as soon as the king had left them on their own, they looked at each other and said, 'How are we going to do that? He's always chopping off people's heads! How can we fill a whole song about how wonderful he is?'

'I know!' said the flute player. 'I'll perform a long flute solo in the middle of the song. That will take up some time.'

The musicians all agreed and began to compose the song immediately.

A few days passed and the day of the party had finally arrived. Everyone was gathered at the palace. The musicians began to get very nervous. No one was more nervous than the flute player. He paced around the room and eventually put his flute down on the floor to get a drink from the buffet table.

But when he walked back to the rest of the musicians, he stepped on his flute, and with a crack the instrument snapped in two.

'Oh no!' exclaimed the flute player. 'Hang on, I might just have time to make a new one!'

The flute player ran down to the riverbank, took out his penknife, cut a reed that was growing there and carved a flute from the reed. He then rushed back to the party, but he had no time to test his flute as the musicians were about to perform their song. King Midas sat on his throne and nodded to the musicians to begin.

The flute player brought the flute to his lips. He blew into it and out came, 'KING MIDAS HAS GOT DONKEY'S EARS!'

The flute player stopped, the musicians gaped, the crowd stared, King Midas glared and said, 'What did you just say?'

'It wasn't me, it was the flute!'

'Take that man away and chop off his head!' barked the king.

'W – W – What?!' stammered the flute player. 'B – B – But it wasn't me!'

The flute player was dragged from the room and the flute was handed to a drummer. The drummer brought the flute to his lips and out came, 'KING MIDAS HAS GOT DONKEY'S EARS!'

'Take that man away and chop off his head too!' barked the king. 'And bring that flute to me!' ordered King Midas.

The drummer was dragged off and the flute was handed to the king. He brought it to his lips, blew into it and out came, 'KING MIDAS HAS GOT DONKEY'S EARS!'

The king leapt in his throne, then shouted, 'How is this possible? I want everyone here questioned until I get answers!'

The king's guards questioned everyone at the party and eventually the barman was brought forward to King Midas.

The barman said, 'Y – Your Majesty. I once met a traveller who said that he had known why you wore a turban. I told him not to tell anyone but rather he should dig a hole in the riverbank and shout the secret into it. That flute was made from a reed that must have grown at the riverbank and held the secret inside of it … until someone blew into it and released the secret for all to hear.'

King Midas thought about this for a moment or two.

Then the barman said, 'We all know your secret now Your Majesty. Can we look at your donkey's ears?'

King Midas paused for a moment and then began to unwrap the turban. The donkey's ears flapped out for all to see.

'Many years ago,' began the king, 'I agreed to judge whose music was the most beautiful: Pan the goat god's music or Apollo the sun god's music. I foolishly declared that Pan's pipes were sweeter sounding than Apollo's lyre. The sun god told me that I was no better judge than a donkey. He gave me these donkey's ears to prove it.'

'I like them,' said the barman. 'I don't like my ears though. They're like handles of a great jug.'

Suddenly someone at the back of the room shouted, 'And I don't like my fingers; they look like spoons!'

Then some else called out, 'I don't like my nose … it's like a bird's beak!'

King Midas realised that we all have things about ourselves that we don't like.

He stopped wearing the turban altogether and let his donkey's ears flap out for all to see. He became a much happier person and the executions stopped altogether.

We live in an image-orientated society where we are constantly being shown the best version of others on social media. This can have an effect on how we view ourselves and others. The next time you look at yourself in the mirror, think of King Midas and intentionally change your attention to the appreciation of what you do like about yourself. This is called 'balanced attention' and helps you to see yourself more positively.

Anansi and the Pot of Knowledge

Anansi is a part spider, part human character from the Ashanti culture in Ghana. He is often portrayed as a trickster, but also acts as an intermediatory between humans and gods. In this tale the knowledge-seeking spider learns the difference between being clever and being wise.

Anansi was so clever that he could spin intricate webs for his home anywhere he went. He was so clever that he could catch his dinner without ever even leaving his home. He was so clever that if his home was destroyed, he could rebuild a perfect copy in only a few hours.

He was clever enough to know that he didn't know *everything*. But he wanted to. He wanted to know all things. He wanted to be the cleverest creature that had ever lived or would ever live. Anansi wanted to know the language of the birds, wanted to know the ways of the trees, wanted to be able to understand all things of this Earth.

So, Anansi scooped up all of the squishy mud that he could. He then moulded this mud into a gigantic pot with a lid for the top. He then left the pot to dry in the sun.

When the pot was hard and firm, Anansi used his web lines to drag the pot around with him; for as well as being very clever, the spider was also very strong.

Anansi travelled the whole of the land asking all creatures to share what they knew with him. He kept this knowledge in his gigantic pot. Before long the pot was filled to the top with knowledge.

Anansi felt satisfied and dragged the pot back to his home. He did not want anyone else to see this gigantic pot of knowledge in case they stole some for themselves.

So, Anansi decided to drag the pot to the top of a tall tree where no one would be able to see the gigantic pot of knowledge among the leafy branches.

When Anansi found the perfect tree, he held on to the gigantic pot with two of his legs and with the other six he began to climb. But the pot was so heavy that Anansi could not grip on to the tree properly. He tried holding on to the pot with one leg and used seven to climb, but he kept dropping the pot before he could climb very far at all. Anansi then tried using different legs for holding and different legs for climbing, but no matter what he did, he just could not manage.

Just then a baby spider came scuttling past.

'Whatcha doing?' asked the baby spider.

'None of your business!' shouted Anansi.

'Are you trying to carry that pot to the top of the tall tree?' smiled the baby spider.

'So what if I am?'

'You'll never do it like that!' laughed the baby spider. 'Why don't you use your web lines? You could tie the pot to your back then use all eight of your legs to climb.'

With that, the baby spider scuttled off.

Anansi rolled his eyes and carried on struggling to get the pot up the tree. But finally he did exactly what the baby spider had suggested; he used his strongest web lines and tied the gigantic pot to his back. It was a struggle but he made it to the top.

Anansi looked at the gigantic pot of knowledge.

He realised that even though he had collected all of this knowledge from all over the land, that baby spider was still wiser than he was.

'I could collect knowledge every day for the rest of my life but there would still be creatures wiser than me,' Anansi said with a shake of his head.

He laughed and kicked the gigantic pot off the branch. It fell from the tall tree and smashed all over the floor. The knowledge then spread all over the world.

'The wisest thing to do is to share knowledge!' he laughed out loud.

Anansi spent the rest of his days listening and sharing knowledge with others to grow wisdom. He always reminded those who wanted to be wise that the best way to learn is to listen.

It's important to recognise that wisdom can come from people of all ages. Taking advice from somebody much younger than yourself might seem counterintuitive, yet intergenerational wisdom sharing, such as sharing practical knowledge or giving advice, can be extremely rewarding for all. The International Journal of Environmental Research and Public Health *conducted a study into intergenerational programmes in 2022 and found that when people spent time with others from different generations, then their overall health and wellbeing was much improved. We can all gain wisdom and feel better by taking the time to listen to people of any age.*

16

The Leprechaun

Leprechauns are known all over the world but originate from Irish folklore. Some consider them to be like fairies and part of the Tuatha Dé Danann, but others believe that leprechaun stories were told by the first natives to Ireland and pre-date any Celtic origin. Unlike fairies, leprechauns are solitary creatures. The name is said to come from 'leath brogan', which means 'shoe maker', while others believe it derives from the word 'luchorpán', which means 'small body'. The shoe-making and small body attributes are now synonymous with leprechaun folklore, as is their mischievous nature and love of trickery and riddles. The following tale is a combination of three separate leprechaun stories into one to show all parts of the leprechaun legend.

Roisin was sitting by the fire listening to her grandfather telling stories of the Tuatha Dé Danann, the first tribes to settle in Ireland. She loved the stories of the battles against the Firbolgs, another Celtic tribe. But in the Battle of Moytura, the Tuatha Dé Danann were victorious. Roisin clapped with glee hearing of the clash of swords, spears and shields in the storytelling.

'Right, come on now,' said her mother. 'I need some help.'

Roisin groaned and protested but she didn't mind helping her mother really.

'What shall I do?' she asked.

'Go and gather some fruit for me, please.'

Gathering a trug woven with willow, she set off away from the house and towards the woods.

'Watch out for the little folk!' her mother called after her.

Fairies? Roisin wasn't scared of them. If she met a fairy then she would be kind and respectful, in return they might give her a reward like a sword made from gold. She might even meet the Goddess Danu who flies with the wind. Roisin was lost in a world of stories as she entered the woods.

The bright bark of the silver birch trees that lined the outside of the woods had glowed in the sunlight, but Roisin was now immersed in a gloomy chill. She ducked under low boughs and stepped skilfully over knotted tangles of roots. Spiderweb strands stroked her skin as she passed ivy-strangled trunks. The smell of earthy soil was immense and there was a taste of fungus that was both bitter and sweet. Her eyes darted from the greens and browns until she saw a cluster of bright red. Her feet flattened some trailing ferns as she approached the berries. Her teeth popped the skin of one and the dark juice was sweet, ripe and delicious. She filled the trug and moved on to another part of the woods.

A huge oak tree with thick roots was surrounded by smaller, more spindly trees. The oak tree stifled the sunlight for the smaller ones. Leaves and bracken crunched under Roisin's feet and then she noticed a trail of smoke that drifted on the air. It was coming from the other side of the tree. She tried to make her approach less obvious. She tiptoed slowly and carefully over the forest floor and peered around the vast tree.

Sitting with his back against the tree was a very small man. It could not have been a child as the man had a thick, long beard and smoked a pipe. The man was wearing green trousers and jacket with a brown leather apron over the top. On his head was a green cocked hat that sat at a strange angle. He had the sole of a shoe in one hand and in the other a grooving tool that he used to shape the sole. He whistled a merry tune as he worked. Roisin was watching him, hypnotised. The man had a variety of tools in his leather apron that he deftly swapped depending on the next job he moved on to. Soon, he was hammering little nails into the sole, attaching it to a tiny, pointed leather shoe he had crafted, all the while puffing on his pipe.

Roisin had been watching for such a long time that she shifted her weight from one foot to another. There was a cracking sound as a twig broke beneath her feet. The man looked up and leapt to his feet in fright.

'Don't be alarmed,' said Roisin with a smile. 'I bid you a very good day, sir. And what a beautiful shoe you have made. Who is it for?'

The man looked at the shoe in his hand as if noticing it for the first time.

'It's for the fairy folk,' he replied with a wry smile. 'They do wear out their shoes quickly with all that dancing.'

'They are lucky to have such a craftsman to make their shoes,' Roisin said.

The man grinned widely. He seemed delighted with the compliment.

'They pay me well with gold.'

'As they should for such beautiful work.'

The grin was now a beaming smile that revealed gleaming white teeth. He leapt up to his feet and put his tools into his apron. The shoe was placed carefully on to some soft leaves.

'What's your name?' he asked.

'Roisin. I'm delighted to meet you.'

'As I am with you. What are you doing in these woods?'

81

'Collecting berries for my mother.'

The man took the pipe out of his mouth and pointed it at the girl.

'You're good to your mother?'

Roisin nodded.

'You listen to what she says?'

She nodded again.

'What do they say about the fairy folk?'

'My grandfather tells me stories about them. You should always treat them with respect. They are older and wiser than us mortals.'

The man clapped his hands with glee.

'Your grandfather is a storyteller?'

Roisin nodded a third time.

'I like you,' the man said. 'I'll tell you what, answer three riddles and you might just get some gold.'

Roisin loved riddles. She and her grandfather swapped them by the fireside most evenings along with the stories. She smiled at the man and looked on with wide eyes and an eager anticipation.

'What goes up and can never go down?'

Roisin's brow furrowed. She stared at the floor lost in thought for a few moments. Then she snapped her eyes back to the man with a smile upon her face.

'Your age!' she announced.

The man gripped his pipe with his teeth and clapped his hands.

'Correct!' he said and did a little jig. 'Next one.'

Roisin's expression was a mask of determination.

'What has to be broken before you can use it?'

The girl looked up at the trees this time with eyes squinted and her nose wrinkled. She remained motionless like that, then looked back to the man.

'An egg?' she asked inquisitively.

The man clapped again.

'Clever girl. Last one.'

Roisin took a step forward and readied herself like she was preparing for a race. She held her breath while she waited for the last riddle. Her mind was tumbling around this way and that. She tried to focus her attention on the here and now, and not think of the gold that she might just get. She tried not to think of what her mother and grandfather would say if she returned with leprechaun gold. She shook her head and stared intently at the man.

'What belongs to you but is used by others?'

With eyes boring into the ancient oak tree, Roisin was a statue in the woods. Her mind raced but her body was frozen solid. Then she did a little jump off the floor and clapped her hands.

'Your name!'

The man clapped too with delight.

'You solved my three riddles!' he declared. 'Good on you!'

Roisin beamed with joy. She looked at the man with eager anticipation.

'You'll be wanting that gold then eh?' he said.

'Yes please!'

'You can find my gold at the end of the next rainbow you see.'

With that, the man collected his shoes and walked off around the tree. Roisin followed him but he had gone. He had disappeared to wherever he lived and could not be followed by mortals. Roisin didn't mind though. She would be rich! Collecting her trug, she ran home to her family to tell them what had happened.

But on the way, it began to rain. It was only a summer shower and soon passed, but then, as the sky cleared, a beautiful rainbow arched its way across the sky. Roisin gasped. There it was! The gold would be waiting for her at the end.

She dropped the trug and ran off chasing the rainbow. She ran and ran and ran. She ran until she could run no more. Then she ran some more. The sky darkened and the rainbow disappeared.

Roisin trudged the many miles back home in darkness and gloom. She had lost her chance to get the leprechaun's gold. She had failed her mother and grandfather.

It was after midnight when Roisin reached her house. Her mother was on the doorstep with a lantern, calling her name. Her grandfather stood beside her with his face a knot of worry.

'There you are!' her mother called and raced towards her.

'Where have you been?' asked her grandfather.

Her mother helped her inside and Roisin sat by the fire, warming her cold bones. With a few tears she told her story. Her grandfather nodded.

'Dear child,' he said. 'Don't you know there is no end to a rainbow?'

'He tricked me?' asked Roisin with wide eyes and a heavy heart.

She went to bed exhausted and tearful. She felt foolish and cheated. Sleep found her at last in the darkness of her room.

In the morning, Roisin's mother woke her up with a shake and a shout.

'Come and see!'

Roisin groaned and slipped out from the bed. Her grandfather had the front door wide open and grinned with excitement.

'Look!' he said, pointing to the porch.

There were three pairs of exquisite shoes waiting for them.

'A gift for your three answers to the riddles!' her mother said.

The leprechaun had rewarded Roisin's cleverness. It wasn't gold, but Roisin was grateful for the shoes. Perhaps they would lead her to the gold when the next rainbow appeared!

The Leprechaun

In this tale, our protagonist solves riddles to earn a prize. Riddle solving might not result in a new pair of shoes for us, but if we exercise our brain regularly it helps our concentration, enables critical thinking, boosts cognitive ability and improves our IQ. By solving riddles, crosswords, word searches and other such problem-solving activities, we are training our brains for the better. We are improving our concentration and boosting our mental capacity.

17

Fafnir the Dragon

The ability to think critically, exercise judgement and adapt to new challenges gives humans a significant advantage in areas such as problem solving, crisis management and decision making. But what would we do to become more intelligent? This tale tells of Odin, the Norse king of the gods, who valued knowledge above all things and wanted to pass on this thirst for wisdom to his children.

Odin, the one-eyed, omniscient king of the gods, lived in the sky city of Asgard. He had plucked out his other eye and dropped it into Mimir's well. This sacrifice had made Odin all-knowing. He understood the way of the world and how it was all balanced and entwined. He knew everything.

Odin had many children in Asgard, including Thor, but he wanted children on Earth too. So, he made Sigurd. A prince on Earth.

Odin did not have time to raise the boy; he was a god and needed in Asgard. So, he commanded that the dwarf blacksmith Regin be the guardian of Sigurd and raise the boy as his own. But Regin was jealous of this boy prince.

'Why should he be getting all of this attention? He doesn't *do* anything. All he does is to strut about telling everyone he's the son of Odin. So what? He's no hero. I'll show everyone on Earth that this boy is weak and puny!'

The next day Regin woke Sigurd early,

'Morning sleepyhead!' smiled Regin. 'Time to get up. You've got a big day ahead of you!'

'Ey … what? Why … what are we doing?' asked a sleepy Sigurd.

'I'm your guardian here on Earth. It's my responsibility to make sure you live up to your title of prince,' Regin began. 'It's time you had your first quest. It's time you started acting like a son of Odin. It's time to slay a dragon!'

Sigurd sat up straight.

'A dragon?'

'The dragon Fafnir!' beamed Regin. 'But first you'll need a sword. I'll get to work straight away.'

Regin went straight to his blacksmith's workshop and Sigurd could hear him hammering away. The noise was deafening but not as deafening as the hammering of Sigurd's own heart in his chest. Nervously, he dressed and arrived in the blacksmith's shop to see Regin holding a *very* hastily made sword out to Sigurd.

'It's a bit light, isn't it?' Sigurd asked as he slashed with the sword this way and that.

'All part of my skill,' grinned Regin.

Sigurd then brought the sword crashing down on to the anvil to test its strength and the sword shattered into a hundred pieces.

'Look what you've done now!' shouted Regin.

'Sorry,' blushed Sigurd.

Regin got to work and again made another very flimsy sword in no time at all. Sigurd began to swing the sword this way and that, then brought it crashing down on the anvil once more. This sword shattered as easily as the first and Regin howled with fury,

'Why do you keep doing that? Of course it will break if you smash an anvil with it!'

'But dragon skin is meant to be tougher to pierce than an anvil,' replied Sigurd. 'I only want to be sure I'm prepared.'

Regin grumbled and made a third sword and presented this quivering weapon to Sigurd.

Sigurd took the sword and said, 'Thanks Regin. Can we go dragon hunting tomorrow? I need to pray to my father and ask for his guidance.'

'I suppose so,' mumbled Regin and skulked off into town to buy some ale.

While he was gone Sigurd tested this third sword on the anvil and again it shattered after just one strike. He didn't want to tell Regin and hurt his guardian's feelings, so Sigurd gathered all of the pieces of the three swords and crafted his own thicker, stronger sword. Sigurd struck the anvil and it split into two. The prince then held the sword aloft and said, 'I shall call you Gram, for you will be my wrath!'

Sigurd then said a prayer to his father, asking for guidance and strength.

The next morning Sigurd was up before Regin and the two set off to the dragon Fafnir's cave. They hid among the rocks and watched as the giant creature slithered out of the dark entrance, stomped a few paces, then took flight looking for its breakfast.

'He's very big, isn't he?' gulped Sigurd.

'It'll be easy,' smiled Regin. 'Just dig a pit near the entrance to the cave. Climb in and hide. When the dragon comes home, he'll walk over the top of you. That's when you open up its belly with that fine sword I made you. The belly is the softest part of the dragon.'

'Great idea!' beamed Sigurd and leapt down to the entrance to Fafnir's cave.

He began digging as fast as he could and in no time was sitting in a large hole waiting for the dragon to return, sword in hand.

Just then an old man peered into the hole. Sigurd saw that the old man had only one eye.

'Hello there young man,' smiled the old man. 'What are you doing?'

Sigurd explained all and the smile faded from the old man's face.

'But if you open Fafnir's belly, his blood will pour into your hole. Dragon's blood is like fire. You'll be burnt alive.

'Tell you what. Why don't you dig another hole? Right next to this one. That way, after you've opened up the dragon's belly, you'll be able to roll into the other hole and be safe from the boiling, burning blood.'

The old man smiled and then disappeared.

Sigurd peered out of his hole but the old man was nowhere to be seen. The prince shrugged and did as he was advised. He dug a second hole and hid back in the first.

Just then, Fafnir came home. As the huge dragon stomped over the top of the hole, Sigurd plunged his sword, Gram, into the scaly belly. He then leapt into the second hole. The dragon roared and collapsed on to the floor, dead. Fafnir's blood poured into the first hole and filled it up to the top. Sigurd leapt from his hole screaming and shouting and cheering. But Regin arrived looking very put out.

'You did it then,' he said glumly.

'Yes!' beamed Sigurd. 'Yes, I did.'

Regin kicked a stone along the floor, then smiled. 'You have done well. So well that we should celebrate. Cut out Fafnir's heart. Cook it over an open fire. I shall eat the heart in your honour and in your name. We'll then travel into town and I'll tell everyone what you have done here today. How does that sound?'

'Fine,' smiled Sigurd. 'You get the fire going and I'll cut out the heart.'

Regin busied himself making the fire while Sigurd used Gram to cut out Fafnir's heart once all of the blood had poured out of the dragon.

'Ale!' cried Regin. 'I need ale with my feast. You cook the heart and I'll get us a few bottles, eh?'

Sigurd smiled and nodded as Regin skipped off to get the ale. As the heart cooked over the fire, the prince stirred it round and round. Some of the juices from the heart splashed on to Sigurd's hand, so he licked them off. As he did, he felt a wave of warmth spread all over his body. He suddenly saw a small bird fly past. It was a wren. A wren with just one eye. It sat on Sigurd's shoulder and whispered in his ear.

'The juices from this heart have made you understand the language of the birds. Imagine what would happen if you ate the whole heart.'

Sigurd nodded and immediately began devouring the dragon heart. As he gulped down the last mouthful, Sigurd became all-knowing. He understood the way of the world and how it was all balanced and entwined. He knew everything. He knew that Regin had been trying to trick him all along.

As his guardian returned, carrying the ale, Sigurd drew Gram and chopped off Regin's head. It rolled into the hole filled with Fafnir's blood and dissolved into nothing.

Sigurd felt ready. Ready to be a warrior. Ready to be a prince. Ready to be Odin's son on Earth.

Imagine the power of knowing all things. What would we give to be omniscient? Is no sacrifice too great in a quest for knowledge? Rather than losing an eye, perhaps it is time that needs to be lost on a journey of wisdom. We need to experience things in order to learn from them. The more we experience, the more we can discover.

18

The Three Crows

This story is another narrative about Jack of beanstalk fame. Here we see our protagonist travelling with a companion who covets Jack's fame and fortune. Coveting what others have can lead to dire consequences, as we shall see here …

Jack and Tom were travelling the land looking for mischief and adventure. Jack hadn't realised this before, but Tom was very jealous of him. Even though Jack had rescued Tom from a giant. Even though Jack had allowed Tom to be a companion on Jack's adventures.

Tom was jealous of the money Jack had gained from the giants he had slain. Jealous of the girls that had kissed Jack once he had freed them from slavery. Jealous of the huge giant's castle that Jack now lived in.

It was Tom who persuaded Jack that they should leave the castle to find him a wife.

They were walking past a murky swamp where old, gnarled trees grew and suddenly Tom whacked Jack over the head with a thick tree branch.

He fell to the floor.

Tom then tied Jack to one of the old, gnarled trees with a strong rope that he had brought with him for exactly this purpose.

Tom plucked out Jack's eyes with his dirty fingernails. He then threw the eyes into the swamp. Jack could only scream as Tom stole the money from Jack's pocket and left him to be eaten by the crows.

Jack was so miserable. Robbed, blinded and left for dead by his best friend. Imagine that!

It was then that he heard the flapping of wings as three crows landed on the tree that he was tied to.

'Have you heard,' spoke the first crow. 'In that city, just behind our swamp, everybody is dying of thirst. Their well has run dry and no one knows what to do. That means *loads* of food for us crows. What they don't know is that there is an underground spring that runs right underneath the market square of that city. If someone was to dig there, they would find enough water for everyone.'

'Have you also heard,' said the second crow. 'The king of that city has a daughter, a princess. She's sick, she's dying and the king is so worried about her that he can think of nothing else. Least of all the people dying of thirst all around him. What he doesn't know is that the toad that lives in this swamp is a magical toad. If you were to burn that toad to ashes, then sprinkle those ashes into water, it would make a magic potion that could cure anything.'

'Human beings,' began the third crow, shaking its head, 'They are *so* stupid.'

With another flapping of wings, the three crows flew away.

Jack had heard every word. He was furiously rubbing his ropes against the old, gnarled tree and was eventually free. He stood. He listened. He heard the croaking of a toad. He moved towards the sound and heard it getting louder. He crept ever closer until he heard the sound at his feet. In a flash, he reached down and had the toad in his hands. He stuffed him into his pocket then felt around on the ground for dried twigs and dead grass. He made a small pile of this and surrounded it with stones. Using the flint from his pocket, Jack then lit a fire and threw the toad on to the fire. Once the fire and the toad had died, he sprinkled the ashes into his water bottle. He shook up the magic potion then dabbed some of it on to his eye sockets.

Instantly Jack's eyes grew back!

'It works!' he shouted.

Whistling a merry tune, he set off for the city. He marched straight up to the palace door and hammered loudly on it.

'I'm here to cure the princess!' Jack announced to the guards.

He was taken to the king. When he heard what Jack was there for, the king looked at him suspiciously.

'You?' the king spluttered. 'A simple lad like you? What makes *you* think that you can cure my daughter when doctors and physicians of every sort have tried and failed?'

'Just let me try,' Jack asked. 'Please!'

He was taken to the princess's bedroom. She was so beautiful!

He gave her some of the magic potion. She instantly sat up, then got up.

'Did you just cure me?' she asked.

'Yes!' Jack beamed at her.

'You're very handsome!' she said.

'And you're very pretty!' Jack replied. 'Would you like to get married?'

'Yeah, go on then!' she smiled back.

They went to see the king.

'I wish to marry your daughter!' Jack announced.

The king gave him a suspicious look once again.

'You may have cured my daughter but do you really think you are worthy of her?' he spluttered.

'I'll tell you what,' Jack said. 'If I can get water for your whole city, will you let me marry your daughter then?'

The king agreed.

Jack collected a shovel from the gardener and marched straight to the market place.

The king, the princess, the gardener, the guards and everyone else in the town followed and watched. Jack lifted up the paving stones and then began to dig.

In no time crystal clear water gushed out in all directions. The king, the princess, the gardener, the guards and everyone was delighted. So was Jack!

The wedding was held straight away and Jack was a married man.

At the wedding reception he was at the top table, chatting away to his new wife, when he noticed Tom sitting at the back of the room, eating, drinking and laughing.

Jack marched straight over to him. When Tom saw that it was none other than Jack, his face fell.

'S – S – Sorry Jack!' he stammered, 'I – Is this your wedding reception? Looks like you've done alright for yourself again!'

'Indeed I have!' Jack laughed. 'And I'm not mad with you.'

Jack patted Tom on the back and pulled him close.

'When you tied me to that tree, plucked out my eyes and left me for the crows, three crows landed on the tree above me. They told me how to cure myself and how I would find my fortune!'

'Really?' gasped Tom. 'Is there any chance you could tie me to that tree, pluck out my eyes and leave me for the crows?'

'Yes!' Jack replied. 'Every chance!'

So off Tom and Jack went.

Jack tied Tom to the tree, plucked out his eyes and left him for the crows. Jack then hid behind a tree beyond and waited.

The flapping of wings could be heard as the three crows landed on the tree that Tom was tied to.

'Have you heard,' spoke the first crow. 'In that city, just behind our swamp, they've found the underground spring. Nobody is dying of thirst. That means no food for us crows.'

'Have you also heard,' said the second crow. 'Someone has cured the king's daughter, the princess. Somebody must have killed that magical toad.'

'I'll bet it was that human being that was tied to the tree earlier,' began the third crow, shaking its head. 'We should have eaten him when we had the chance.'

'Well, we won't be making that mistake again, will we?' said the three crows together.

There was another flapping of wings as the crows descended. Jack heard Tom's screams all the way back to the palace.

Whenever we have been hurt by somebody, our initial reaction might be to take revenge in some way. However, in Michael Price's book Revenge and the People Who Seek It *he states, 'Studies have found that while there may be initial satisfaction, revenge actually perpetuates the pain of the original offence.' So perhaps Jack might have been better off following a path to forgiveness and understanding, not only for Tom's benefit, but also for his own.*

19

The Parables of the Lotus Sutra

The Lotus Sutra contains seven profound parables, each imparting a distinct lesson. The use of seven parables holds special symbolic significance, as the number seven is regarded as auspicious in many cultures, including Buddhism. Indeed, the number is significant in many folk tales, from seven dwarves to seven ravens to seven goat kids.

The Lotus Sutra parables can be compared to the seven chakras, the seven days of the week or the seven colours of the rainbow. While each parable conveys a unique message, together they all illuminate the power of Buddha's nature.

Here we see all seven parables …

Parable of the Blazing House

A wealthy man was on his way home from a business trip. Excitement welled inside him. He would see his children very soon! He arrived home to his large mansion only to find smoke bellowing and flames roaring from the downstairs windows. Were his children still inside?

He raced to the front door but his way was blocked by a roaring fire. He looked up and heard his children playing in one of the bedrooms on the upper floor.

'Children!' the man yelled. 'Get out while you can!'

But the children were too busy playing with their toys and didn't want to leave.

'We're playing,' they called. 'Leave us alone, Dad.'

'You must leave! The house is on fire! Quickly, before it's too late!'

'We told you,' the children went on. 'We're playing with our toys.'

The man raced over to get a ladder. He pushed it against the house, next to the bedroom window where his children played.

'If you climb down this ladder you can play with some new toys. They're even better than any toys you have ever had before!'

The children suddenly stopped playing and appeared at the window. They started to climb down to safety.

'Where are the toys?' they asked once down the ladder.

The wealthy man was delighted to see his children safely away from the blaze.

'Here,' smiled the man. 'This is your gift.'

A beautiful white ox cart stood next to the man. The children climbed inside and settled down. There they sat with contentment and joy.

In this parable the wealthy man symbolises the Buddha, while his children represent humanity. The burning house signifies samsara, which is the cycle of birth and death that is filled with suffering. The toys inside the house, which captivate the children, symbolise worldly distractions that keep us entangled in samsara. The toys promised by the Buddha to his followers are the rewards for adhering to his teachings, with the beautiful white ox cart representing true liberation or enlightenment.

Parable of the Lost Son

There was once the son of a rich man. The son decided to leave his father's house and travel the country. He wanted to see what life was really like outside of the gilded cage he currently lived in. So, the boy went from town to town, city to city and village to village. The little money and food he had with him was soon gone and he began to beg for food and water. The boy began to suffer greatly and finally concluded that he was worthless and his life served no purpose.

Meanwhile, the rich man missed his son. He wondered what adventures he might be having on his travels. Years had passed and the rich man had grown older. The palace home looked very different too. There were new towers and the whole building had been extended several times.

One day, the son arrived at his father's palace. He didn't recognise the place and asked for a job, any job, in return for food and shelter. The servants hired the boy to clean the bathrooms in the palace. The boy felt that this job would be suitable as it matched his now lowly status. So, he accepted the job and unknowingly went to work in his former home, cleaning the toilets and scrubbing the floors.

The rich man saw his son cleaning the floors. He was delighted and wanted to embrace his son but didn't want to scare the boy away. Instead, the rich man disguised himself as a servant and set to work cleaning and scrubbing side by side with his son. The rich man saw how hard his son worked. He was filled with joy and love that his son had become such a diligent worker.

The rich man enjoyed his time with his son, but one day the father became so ill that he was taken to his bed. There he remained for weeks and it became clear that he would soon die. The rich man knew that this should be the time to reveal his identity to his son. He called for him and told the boy that he was his father. Father and son embraced. Then the rich man died. He left his entire estate and wealth to his son.

In this parable, the father represents the Buddha and his son represents his followers. The son leaving home and living in poverty mirrors our own spiritual wandering and suffering. The simple jobs the son carries out symbolise the Buddha's teachings and practices and his joy in such menial tasks represents his (and our) spiritual progress. The father's inheritance is the teaching of the Law of Supreme Perfect Enlightenment.

The Parable of the Medicinal Herbs

Just at the beginning of the monsoon season, when the ground was parched and dry, the earth yearned for rain. The plants longed for moisture, the soil craved the rain. Eventually, the clouds grew brooding and dark, then finally released a downpour of fat and round raindrops. The rain fell and the soil, trees, grass and the plants were grateful.

But all of the plants were varied and all different sizes and shapes. As such, each received the rain in a different way. Some had roots that were shallow while others went down deep into the ground. These roots that went down deep weren't reliant on the surface water that would evaporate quickly. The plants with the shallow roots are often left thirsty and wilting as the water comes and goes. The plants with the deeper roots find constant cool refreshment from deep within the earth.

The clouds during the monsoon season give generously but also equally to all of the plants of the earth. But it is the different ways that these plants absorb this moisture that allows some to grow more successfully than others.

In this story, the different types of plants represent humans and the rain symbolises the Buddha's teachings. All plants receive the rain but each absorbs it differently. Similarly, people receive the Buddha's teachings, but how they absorb and apply them determines the kind of person they become.

This parable teaches us that even though everyone receives the same teachings from the Buddha, not all benefit from them in the same way. The way we absorb and practise these teachings can help to shape our spiritual development.

The Parable of the Imaginary City

There was a caravan of travellers who journeyed across a desert searching for treasure. Their leader was wise and they rested often, but despite this the travellers were becoming more exhausted by the day. They were also becoming doubtful that the treasure actually existed. The wearied and disillusioned travellers began to slow to a snail's pace. Many of the travellers didn't have the strength to carry on and wanted to turn around and go back home.

'There is a city not far from here,' the wise leader announced. 'There is fresh water, good food and clean beds!'

This gave the travellers the motivation they needed to continue, so on they went. With their spirits lifted, the group made good progress.

Finally, the group arrived at the city. There they stopped and rested, as the wise leader had promised. But when they felt better, the city suddenly vanished. At one moment it was there and the next it was gone. The travellers were amazed and looked to their leader to explain. 'The city is not real,' the wise leader admitted. 'It was a creation from your imagination. But it has satisfied your needs and has served its purpose. It has given you the strength to continue on your quest.'

The travellers moved on and found the treasure nearby shortly afterwards.

The wise caravan leader in this parable represents the Buddha, who guides his followers. The caravan is in search of treasure, symbolising Buddha-nature, while the imaginary city where they stop for temporary respite represents provisional nirvana. The lesson in this parable is that the disciples of the Buddha might be tempted to view achieving nirvana as their ultimate goal. However, the Buddha warns that this is only a temporary state and that they should not be content with it. Their ultimate aspiration should be Buddhahood. Thus, the Buddha encourages his disciples to strive for their highest potential, as long as they are willing to follow him and continue on the path.

The Parable of the Jewel in the Robe

There was once a man who had lost everything he had owned. He lost his job, which led to him losing his house. He had no money or food. He wandered the streets begging for the scraps that others did not want. Eventually, the poor man decided to go and visit an old friend who was very wealthy to ask her for help. The poor man knocked at the rich friend's door. The house was very grand indeed. The poor man stood back to admire the home when the door was opened and the rich friend saw the poor man.

'Oh my goodness!' she gasped. 'Come inside, quickly!'

The poor man went in and sat by the fire. The rich friend gave the poor man plate after plate of fine food, followed by a bottle of sumptuous wine. The poor man devoured the food and gulped the wine. The rich friend opened a second bottle and the poor man drank this too. Soon, he was slumped on a soft chair and snoring loudly.

The wealthy woman let her friend sleep, but in the morning she had to leave on business. Before she left, she went to her safe and found a priceless gem. She decided to hide it in the poor man's robe as a present. She sewed it into the lining of the robe so that it would be a surprise for her friend when he finally woke up.

The wealthy woman left on her trip and the poor man woke up sometime later. He stretched and, feeling a little fuzzy headed, went on a walk to reflect on the kindness of his friend. He walked through the park and enjoyed the day but knew that he had to try and get some work. He had to somehow rebuild his life.

The following days were hard. The poor man met rejection after rejection. Once again he found himself begging for food and sleeping in the streets.

This carried on until one day he bumped into his good friend. She was shocked to see the man as poor as he was before.

'But what of the priceless gem I gave to you?' she asked.

The poor man did not know what she was talking about. So, she showed him the gem that was sewed into the poor man's robe.

'This has been there the whole time?' asked the man with wide eyes and an even wider mouth.

Even though the gem had always been with him, he had no idea it had been there. Now he was able to sell it and free himself from the grip of poverty.

In this parable, the rich friend represents the Buddha, while the poor man symbolises us. The precious jewel sewn into the man's robe stands for the Buddha's teachings about the truth of Buddha-nature. Just like the poor man always had the gem with him, sewn into his robe lining even if he didn't know it, everybody always has the Buddha's teachings about Buddha-nature within them. By following the Buddha's teachings, we can all achieve Supreme Perfect Enlightenment.

The Parable of the Precious Pearl in the Topknot

There was once a king who was extremely rich. He had a treasure room in his palace that was filled with gold, silver, emeralds, sapphires, rubies, diamonds and many other precious metals and stones. The king would reward his soldiers when they returned from battle victorious with a golden coin each. Those who had been particularly valiant and brave received a precious gem of some sort. But there was a very special treasure that the king kept hidden from all. This was a precious pearl that gleamed like a tiny moon, cradling the secrets of the sea in its smooth, iridescent embrace. Whenever the king admired the pearl it shimmered with an ethereal glow, as if it held the light of a thousand sunsets within its lustrous core. He kept this precious pearl hidden in his topknot, away from the sight of others.

So the years passed, until the king heard of a truly brave soldier's deeds. This soldier had proven his worth in the constant fight against the many evils of the kingdom. His relentless loyalty and courage needed a very special reward. So, the king gave the soldier the precious pearl from his topknot. The object that was a sliver of Heaven in the form of a pearl.

In this story, the wise king represents the Buddha, while his followers are the soldiers. The gifts that the king bestows upon his army are the preliminary teachings of Buddhism, whereas the pearl in the topknot is the Law of Supreme Perfect Enlightenment.

To receive the Buddha's highest teachings, we must first practise his fundamental teachings in our everyday lives. Only then, when the time and conditions are just right, will we be ready to receive the pearl of supreme enlightenment.

The Parable of the Skilful Doctor

Long ago there lived a very skilled doctor who knew how to blend herbs to make medicine for any ailment. Any illness her patients had, the doctor was able to find the cure. She travelled far and wide across the land and became the most sought-after expert in medicines of every kind.

One day, when she was away helping the sick in the towns nearby, her children went into her office and found one of her medicine chests. They prised the chest open and inside found some tablets, made from a blend of many herbs. These tablets were emerald green and looked like the sweetest of sweets. The children ate the tablets and soon became very sick.

The doctor was sent for and she rushed back home. By now the children were gravely ill. They held their abdomens, wailing and groaning with stomach pains. The doctor rushed to her office and found the open medicine chest. After a speedy inventory, she established which tablets had been taken and then selected the antidotes. She raced back to her children and offered them the tablets. These too were made from herbs and looked the same as the tablets that had made them sick.

Two of her children took the medicine immediately and were almost instantly cured. But her other two children refused the medicine even when their mother begged them to take the tablets. They would not listen to her as they were convinced that these tablets would surely kill them.

The doctor did not know what to do. She didn't want to force the tablets down her children's throats, so instead came up with a plan. She left the medicine with the children, reminding them that these tablets were the only things that would cure them, then set off to the next town.

When she got there, the doctor sent a messenger to see the children to tell them that she had died.

The children wept and mourned the loss of their wise and skilled mother. It was in this state of grieving that the children decided to take the medicine as their mother had instructed.

'It was the last thing she wanted us to do,' the poorly pair said. 'We should at least try the tablets.'

So, they took the medicine and were cured of their pain. Upon hearing that the children were now cured and recovered from the poison, the doctor came back home and was reunited with all of her children, who were now well, as she was too.

In this parable, the wise doctor who creates the antidote to save her children represents the Buddha. The poison the children ingested symbolises our ignorance and delusions, while the antidote is the Buddha's teachings.

The children who refuse to take the medicine represent those who reject the Buddha's teachings, even when they are suffering. In contrast, the children who take the medicine represent those who are willing to listen to the Buddha and apply his teachings. If we are willing to listen to him and put his teachings into practice, we can be saved from our suffering.

The seven parables represent the Buddha's teachings and how they can be applied to life. Each story illustrates a different aspect of the Dharma (the truth). Together, they form the Law of Supreme Perfect Enlightenment, as a guide for Buddhists on their journey towards liberation.

20

King Sisyphus

A Sisyphean task is defined as a seemingly endless and futile task that you keep trying to do but it never gets done. The word comes from the name of King Sisyphus, who is punished in a most unusual way ...

King Sisyphus was a man of extraordinary intellect, his mind as sharp as the edge of a well-forged falcata. He possessed an uncanny ability to observe and listen with an intensity that left nothing unnoticed. The king rarely spoke, but when he did his words were meticulously chosen and invariably accurate.

Sisyphus was also very, very wealthy. His palace was adorned with the finest vases, plates and statues. His clothes were intricately decorated and his crown was unrivalled. He also had a herd of cattle whose beauty was known far and wide. These cows were magnificent creatures; their horns polished to a silver gleam, their hides a rich, deep red and the bells around their necks producing music so enchanting it could soothe the wildest of beasts.

Nearby lived Autolycus, the earthly son of Hermes. He was gifted with his father's swiftness and was the fastest runner on Earth. He could cover 50 miles in less than ten minutes during his morning jogs around the palace grounds.

Autolycus had heard not only of Sisyphus' herd of cows but also of the king's renowned observational skills and intelligence. With a mischievous grin, Autolycus decided to put them to the test. He transformed his own modest garden into a makeshift pasture and prepared a vast bucket of white dye. Late at night, he darted into the palace grounds, snatching one of Sisyphus' prized cows and whisking it away to his home. There, he dyed the cow from red to white and repeated the process until six of the king's cattle grazed in his garden.

The next morning, as King Sisyphus strolled through his grounds, his keen eyes quickly noted the missing cows. He questioned his farmers, but they were as bewildered as he was. Meanwhile, Autolycus continued his nightly raids, each time leaving Sisyphus' herd six cows fewer. Despite suspicions falling on Autolycus, none dared accuse the son of Hermes without firm evidence. Sisyphus' farmers were ordered to watch day and night but Autolycus managed to sneak past them using his swift speed, going unnoticed even when carrying each cow!

However, the clever king devised a cunning plan to catch Autolycus red-handed, or rather, white-handed.

The following morning, King Sisyphus knocked on Autolycus' door.

'You have my cattle in your garden,' the king declared.

'I don't know what you mean,' Autolycus replied, with a slight smile.

Sisyphus and his guards marched past Autolycus into the garden filled with white cows.

'My cows are red, and yours are white,' Autolycus said smoothly.

Sisyphus said nothing, but approached the nearest cow and lifted its hoof, revealing an inscription: 'These cows belong to King Sisyphus.'

Everyone gasped and stared at Autolycus.

King Sisyphus roared with laughter. 'Oh, well done, Autolycus! You almost had me there. I haven't had such fun in ages. Come back to my palace; we'll eat, drink, and make merry!'

And so, Sisyphus and Autolycus returned to the palace, where a grand feast lasted for many days. The king and Autolycus became fast friends, and Sisyphus' daughter fell in love with Autolycus at first sight. They were married a few days later, and the celebrations continued. Years later, they would have a son named Odysseus, who would become one of the greatest heroes of all time.

But for now, once the feasting was over, Sisyphus' daughter and Autolycus moved into a home of their own. King Sisyphus, however, grew bored once more. He resumed his habit of watching and listening, making it *his* business to know *everyone else's* business. He lurked behind large vases, eavesdropped on private conversations.

One day, while skulking outside his palace, he noticed the sea nymph Aegina running from the beach into a nearby cave. Sisyphus hid behind a rock and watched as Zeus, king of the gods, descended from Mount Olympus on a cloud. Zeus looked around cautiously before disappearing into the cave with Aegina.

Sisyphus, thrilled with this juicy piece of gossip, hurried home, eager to use it to his advantage.

The next morning, Asopus, the river god and father of Aegina, visited King Sisyphus, his face a mask of anger.

'I know you see all things, King Sisyphus,' Asopus boomed. 'My daughter Aegina disappears every day and refuses to tell me where she goes or with whom. Tell me if you know, and I will reward your land with fresh flowing water for every home.'

Sisyphus smiled, relishing the knowledge he possessed. He told Asopus everything.

Furious, Asopus rushed to the beach, just in time to see Zeus flying back to Mount Olympus and Aegina emerging from the cave. Enraged, Asopus hurled a magic spell at his daughter, transforming her into an island, which grew to become one of the most beautiful in Greece.

Zeus, heartbroken and furious, vowed revenge on the meddling king. He summoned his messenger, Hermes, and sent him to the underworld to fetch his brother Hades.

Hades, god of the dead, was not pleased to be summoned to the sunlit realm of Olympus. However, he listened as Zeus ordered him to find King Sisyphus and drag him to Tartarus, to make him suffer for his betrayal.

Hades agreed, eager to return to his dark domain. He flew to King Sisyphus' palace, but the king was prepared. Knowing Zeus would seek vengeance, Sisyphus had planned accordingly. When Hades arrived, Sisyphus greeted him with feigned hospitality.

'You know why I am here,' Hades said wearily, rubbing his forehead. 'Come with me.'

But Sisyphus threw open the curtains, flooding the room with blinding sunlight. Hades, struck by a severe headache, was momentarily weakened. Sisyphus seized the opportunity, binding Hades with a long rope and escaping to the cave that had once been Zeus and Aegina's secret meeting place.

As night fell, Hades recovered and returned to the underworld, furious and humiliated. He tasked Hermes with capturing Sisyphus and bringing him to Tartarus. Hermes, glad to leave the gloomy underworld, quickly located Sisyphus disguised as a beggar and dragged him back to Hades.

However, to cross the River Styx, the king had to pay the ferryman with a gold coin. Dressed as a beggar, Sisyphus had no money. The ferryman refused him passage, forcing Hermes to return Sisyphus to his palace.

Hades was furious. He instantly returned to the palace and found the king sitting smugly on his throne. Wasting no time, Hades captured Sisyphus and dragged him to Tartarus, presenting him with a massive boulder at the base of an enormous mountain.

'Push this boulder to the top and I will let you go,' Hades decreed.

Sisyphus, his heart heavy with dread, began the strenuous task. He pushed and strained for days, but just as he neared the summit, the boulder rolled back to the bottom. Again and again, Sisyphus struggled, only to see his efforts undone each time.

And so, as far as anyone knows, King Sisyphus remains in Tartarus to this day, eternally pushing his boulder, a symbol of his cleverness turned to foolishness.

Here we have another cautionary tale, a warning not to let our gifts become our undoing. Many historical figures have fallen due to their talents. For instance, Julius Caesar's exceptional strategic mind and ambition ultimately led to his assassination by those who feared his power. Our talents are gifts that enrich not only our lives but also the lives of those around us. They enhance our own lives but also contribute to the greater good. Yet, if not used with wisdom, they can also be our downfall.

21

The Hodja and the Donkey

Nasruddin (sometimes spelled Nasreddin) Hodja was known as 'the Wise Fool'. The stories about him are often ridiculous but matters are always settled amicably.

The oldest Nasruddin Hodja story appears in the book Saltukname, *written in 1480, which also includes other folk tales. According to* Saltukname, *Hodja was born in Sivrihisar, a town whose residents were renowned for their eccentric behaviour and ingenuity. However, it should be noted that these stories are not directly related to Hodja himself or his historical persona. In other words, over the centuries, many new tales featuring him as the main character have emerged.*

Annually, from 5–10 July, the International Nasruddin Hodja Festival is held in Akşehir, the location of his tomb. To keep the character of the Hodja alive, Turkish writers and artists have incorporated him into various forms of art, including drama, music, movies comic strips and paintings. He is perhaps Islam's best-known trickster character.

In this absurdly silly narrative, I have combined two Hodja folk tales to give a taste of the misadventures of the protagonist.

One morning, Nasruddin Hodja was cleaning the dishes in the kitchen. He looked out the window to admire the sunrise. A huge branch from an old tree was blocking his view.

'This is no good at all,' the Hodja muttered to himself. 'It needs to go.'

He grabbed a ladder and a saw, then stomped up to the tree. He leaned his ladder against the trunk and climbed up. He then sat on the offensive branch and began to saw. As he did, the branch began to sway and wobble.

Just then, a young girl walked along the path that led to town. The girl stopped when she saw the Hodja.

'What are you doing Nasruddin Hodja?' the girl asked. 'You'll fall when you cut that branch!'

The Hodja dismissed the warning with a sniff and a wave of his hand.

'Do you think I have never sawed a branch before? I know what I'm doing!'

With a shrug, the girl continued on her way and Hodja resumed sawing. He sawed and sawed until, sure enough, the branch gave way. The Hodja tumbled to the ground with a thud. He rubbed his head a few times and then sat up.

'That girl predicted I would fall! She knows the future. She must be a real sage. Surely, such a wise child such as that could tell me how many more years I'll live!'

The Hodja scrambled to his feet and chased after the girl. His sandals were a blur of dust and stones until, at last, he caught up with the girl.

'You there! You who can predict the future. You knew I was going to fall so maybe you can tell me how many more years I'll live?'

The girl looked puzzled at first and then a slow smile began to creep across her face.

'Well, now,' she pondered rubbing her chin. 'You will die … when your donkey farts three more times.'

The Hodja gasped. His donkey was a particularly flatulent creature. He needed to sell it right away. If he had no donkey then he would live forever!

'Thank you oh wise one!'

The words were barely from the Hodja's mouth and he bounded back to his home. He ran straight around the back, untied the donkey and began to hurriedly lead the animal to the market. He had to sell the beast quickly or he was doomed.

As the Hodja and the donkey trotted beside one another there was a faint, almost imperceptible hiss, like air escaping from a balloon. As the sound grew louder, it turned into a sputtering noise, reminiscent of an old engine struggling to start. The burst of air resonated with a quick, sharp note, followed by a lingering, low rumble that gradually faded into silence. The Hodja gasped, and not because a faint, slightly sulphurous odour began to fill the air.

'Oh no! That's one already.'

The Hodja pulled at the donkey's rein even harder to hurry the animal along but this only led to further flatulence.

'That's two!'

Immediately a third and high-pitched tooting came from the donkey.

'That's it then,' the Hodja sighed, 'I'm done for.'

He became convinced that this was his end so he lay down on the ground, for he supposed that's what the dead should do.

Hours crept by as slowly as an acorn becomes an oak. The Hodja sighed long and hard.

'Being dead is so boring.'

A short while after this, some villagers happened upon him lying there.

'Nasruddin Hodja has died!'

With great solemnity, they lifted him up on to a wagon that they were taking to get supplies from the market. They gently placed the Hodja on this wagon and began to take him to the cemetery for burial.

As they made their way, they reached a crossroads and started to argue about which direction to take. One insisted they go left, while another argued for the right path.

'The left path is short and the right takes forever!'

'But the left path is covered in stones and the right one is smooth.'

The disagreement went on for some time, so eventually the Hodja opened his eyes, sat up and said calmly, 'Well, if it was up to me then I would prefer the right path so that I don't feel every bump in the road.'

The villagers shrieked in terror and fled as fast as they could.

The Hodja sat for a while but then thought it was best if he lay back down.

Meanwhile, the donkey had grown restless so wandered back up the road to its home. When the Hodja's wife saw the donkey wandering with a limp rein, she thought she had better see where her husband had got to.

She followed the donkey's hoof prints on the sandy road and finally found her husband laid upon a wagon.

'What are you doing on that?' she asked the Hodja.

'I'm dead.'

'What?' she said with a sigh.

The Hodja sat up once more and explained, 'Our donkey farted three times, so I died.'

'You soon will be dead if you don't get home and finish those dishes, silly old fool.'

With that, the Hodja and his wife returned home.

This absurd tale reflects the humour of the Hodja stories. They were meant to entertain but also to help us ponder on life's big questions. In this tale the Hodja wishes to know how long he has left to live so much that he is willing to believe a child's trick. He longs for eternal life so much that he thinks he can trick his way into immortality by selling his donkey. Our own desire for immortality is perhaps a direct response to the fear of death. Many of us are afraid of dying. If we were immortal, we could avoid both that fear and its cause. Therefore, the desire for immortality is essentially a desire to avoid death.

22

Orpheus and Eurydice

This famous tale from Ancient Greece is a tragic story of love and loss. Yet, it also contains the power of undying hope. It is a story of endurance and persistence. It's also just a great story.

Orpheus was a musician of unparalleled talent, his melodies so exquisite that they could make the very stars pause in their celestial dance. He plucked his string kithara with grace, he played his tortoiseshell chelys lyre with skill and blew the double-reeded aulos so that each note seemed to sing with the voice of the gods. His own voice, rich and resonant, wove through the air like a golden thread, enchanting all who heard it.

One day, as Orpheus wandered through an ancient forest, his song rose like a lark's call at dawn, filling the woods with its ethereal beauty. In the distance, he spotted a group of girls, their laughter tinkling like silver bells as they played among the trees. Undeterred, he continued singing, each note a beacon drawing him closer. These were no ordinary girls; they were wood nymphs, mystical beings capable of transforming from maiden to tree and back again at will.

As Orpheus neared, the nymphs, startled by his presence, gasped and morphed into slender trees, their leaves trembling.

All but one. This wood nymph, named Eurydice, stood rooted in place, captivated by the musician's presence. Her smile, shy yet radiant, mirrored the sun breaking through morning mist.

'Hello,' Orpheus greeted her, his voice a caress.

'Greetings,' Eurydice replied softly, her cheeks tinged with the blush of dawn.

'You're very pretty,' Orpheus said, his own face flushing with admiration.

'You're very handsome,' Eurydice responded, her bright eyes sparkling.

They talked and talked and eventually decided that they could not be parted. Their love was so instant and passionate that they decided to marry.

Their decision made, they climbed to the top of a hill, seeking the favour of the gods of Olympus. In a blaze of light and a clap of thunder, Hera, queen of the gods, materialised before them. She glowed with a brilliance that rivalled the midday sun, her smile a cascade of light. With a voice like the ringing of a thousand golden bells, she declared them husband and wife, then vanished as suddenly as she had appeared.

Orpheus and Eurydice, now bound by love and divine decree, were overjoyed.

'We're married!' they exclaimed in unison, their voices blending in perfect harmony.

'Play me some music! Sing me a song! I want to dance!' Eurydice urged, her joy overflowing.

Orpheus nodded, picking up his lyre, and began to play. He sang too as Eurydice twirled and danced. Her movements were as fluid and graceful as a stream in spring. But suddenly, she stumbled, a sharp pain shooting through her leg. She looked down to see a snake slithering away, its venom already coursing through her veins. She fell, her body lifeless, her spirit fleeing before Orpheus could reach her.

'No!' Orpheus cried, his voice breaking like a wave upon the rocks. 'We've only just been married, and now she's gone!'

Determined to reclaim his love, he vowed, 'I will travel to the edge of the world! I will descend into the Underworld! I will face Hades himself and bring her back!'

Clutching his lyre, Orpheus set off on his epic journey over vast landscapes. Days turned into nights and nights into days until he finally reached the River Styx at the edge of the world. Its waters were smooth as glass, glowing with an eerie, dark luminescence. A boat emerged from the mists, guided by a figure cloaked in black. As Charon the Ferryman drew near, his hood fell back, revealing a skeletal visage with hollow, staring eyes.

'May I cross?' Orpheus asked, his voice steady but his heart pounding.

The skull nodded, and Orpheus climbed aboard. They glided silently across the river, arriving at the gates of Tartarus that were massive and foreboding. Orpheus stepped on to the shadowed shore, nodding his thanks to the ferryman. A menacing growl rumbled behind him. He turned to a colossal three-headed dog with the tail of a snake that hissed and writhed. Each head bared fangs like daggers, foam dripping from their snarling mouths.

'Cerberus!' Orpheus gasped. 'Oh mighty guardian of the Underworld, who never sleeps but endures endless sentry of Tartarus, I dedicate this song to you.'

With trembling hands, he began to strum his lyre, singing a lullaby so soothing it seemed to weave a spell. Cerberus' eyelids drooped and soon the monstrous hound lay asleep. The beast slept for the first time since its creation. Thousands of years of service were now lost in dream-filled bliss. Orpheus slipped past the hellhound, his song a soft whisper in the shadowed halls.

The Underworld was a realm of mist and shadow, ghosts flitting like whispers through the gloom. Orpheus pressed on, his path lit only by the faint glow of the spirits. At last, he reached the heart of the Underworld, where Hades sat upon a throne of bones, his eyes as cold and dark as the void.

'What do you seek, living man?' Hades demanded, his voice like the echo of death.

'I've come for my wife, Eurydice,' Orpheus pleaded. 'We were only just married, and she was taken from me. Please, let me bring her back.'

'No,' Hades replied, his tone final.

'Please?' Orpheus implored.

'No.'

'I beg you!' Orpheus' voice cracked with desperation as he fell to his knees.

'No.'

Heartbroken but resolute, Orpheus began to sing, pouring all his love and sorrow into his music. His song was a haunting lament that resonated through the Underworld, drawing the spirits close. Even Hades, unmoved by centuries of suffering, felt a tear escape and fall to the ground.

'I know the pain of separation,' Hades said quietly. 'My wife, Persephone, is with me for only three months of the year.'

He sighed deeply. 'Alright, you may have her back.'

Orpheus leapt up as joy flooded his heart.

'But,' Hades warned, 'you must not look at her until you have crossed the Styx back to the human world. If you do, she will be lost to you forever.'

'Thank you, I understand,' Orpheus vowed.

Filled with hope, Orpheus began the journey back, his steps light with anticipation. He passed the sleeping Cerberus, who seemed to smile in his slumber. Orpheus then crossed the gates, but doubts gnawed at him. Was Eurydice truly following him? Had she even left the Underworld? The urge to look back was overwhelming, but he resisted, focusing on the path ahead.

As he neared the river, he could no longer bear the uncertainty. The ferryman awaited him, and Orpheus' resolve crumbled. He turned to see Eurydice, her ghostly form shimmering behind him. In that instant, she was pulled back into Tartarus, her spirit vanishing like mist in the dawn.

Devastated, Orpheus crossed the river with Charon, then sat alone on the opposite shore with his lyre. He played the saddest song ever heard, his grief pouring out in every note. He neither ate nor drank, singing of his lost love until he himself faded from the world.

In death, Orpheus returned to the Underworld, reunited at last with Eurydice. Together, they embraced in the realm of shadows, their spirits intertwined for eternity. And so, in a bittersweet twist, they died happily ever after.

This tale follows a theme of eternal love that intertwines with desperation, highlighting both the beauty and risks of deep devotion. Orpheus's journey to reclaim Eurydice shows the lengths love can inspire, but also the dangers of holding on too tightly. His inability to let go of her becomes a cautionary tale, suggesting that while love can be a source of strength, it can also threaten wellbeing when one cannot move forward. This story serves as a reflection on the balance between cherishing love and preserving one's mental health.

Cerberus's role in this story also reminds us of a valuable lesson. As he finally falls into slumber, we are reminded that sleep does not come easily for some of us. We do not have Orpheus to sing us lullabies, yet sleep is crucial for both mental and physical health.

Sleep impacts the regulation of emotions, reducing the risk of mood swings, irritability, and emotional instability, which perhaps explains Cerberus' initial response to a visitor at the gate! Poor sleep is even linked to mental health disorders like depression and anxiety. Adequate sleep helps manage stress and emotional resilience.

23

The Phoenix

In Greek mythology the phoenix was associated with the sun and was seen as a symbol of the cycle of life and death. In Egyptian mythology, the Bennu was a type of phoenix that represented the soul and the idea of creation and rebirth. Fenghuang is often referred to as the Chinese phoenix, symbolising harmony, balance and prosperity. However, this Vietnamese folk tale focuses on a different aspect of the phoenix: that of love.

Deep in the heart of the forested highlands, where the mist clung to the hillsides and the air hummed with life, there stood a tree unlike any other. It was a giant among giants and seemed as if it had been there since time itself began. No one knew how many centuries had etched their mark on its bark, but the tree's massive trunk was as wide as the arm span of twenty people, its surface rough and gnarled, weathered by countless seasons.

The tree's roots, ancient and thick, snaked out from the base like a thousand serpents, pushing up through the earth with the strength of mountains, spreading in all directions to a radius of many metres. These roots had woven themselves into the very fabric of the forest floor, binding soil and stone alike, as if to remind the earth that this tree was its eternal guardian. Its bark, dark and furrowed, was as hard as iron. High above, its colossal branches reached out like the arms of a benevolent giant, cradling the nests of countless birds. These branches were alive with the fluttering of wings and harmonious songs.

Beneath the protective shadow of the tree, the earth was always cool, a quiet sanctuary from the heat of the sun. It was a place where the creatures of the forest came to rest, a natural cathedral where the morning light filtered through the leaves like the glow of stained glass, soft and sacred.

Each morning, as the first light of dawn broke over the horizon, the birdsong filled the air with a melody that echoed through the forest. In the great tree, high up in the branches, there was an opening as large as a grapefruit. It was 12 metres above the ground. This hidden chamber contained a small, golden egg. No one knew how the egg had come to be there. The egg was a mystery, its origins known only to the tree and the forest that surrounded it.

Thirty years passed and still the egg remained, untouched and intact. However, when the sky was dark and the wind whispered through the leaves, the birds would be startled from their sleep by a strange light. It was a brilliant glow that emanated from the golden egg. The birds, though fearful, could not help but gaze in wonder.

Finally, one night, under a full moon so bright it seemed to turn the forest to silver, the golden egg began to crack. A tiny, strange bird emerged into the cold night with a crying chirp. The bird's cry echoed through the forest and she continued to call out until the first rays of sunlight broke through the canopy, heralding the morning. As the symphony of birds began anew, the little bird fell silent and listened.

The bird grew quickly. Mother birds brought her nuts and grains, placing them carefully in the opening of the tree. The bounty was always more than enough, and soon she taught herself to fly, her wings beating softly against the dawn, and she gathered sticks and straw to build a new nest in the tree.

The egg had been golden and the bird matched the colour. But she was also covered with feathers of scarlet, amber and saffron. Her wingspan was vast and she flew with a grace that was almost otherworldly, moving slowly and silently through the skies.

She often wondered where she had come from but none of the creatures of the forest seemed to know.

Beside the ancient forest stood a small, weathered hut, home to a solitary monk who had lived there for nearly fifty years. The bird often flew near to the hut, where she would see the monk walking slowly down the path to the spring to collect water.

One day, as the bird watched from the skies high above, she noticed two monks walking together along the same path. That night, perched in the branches of a nearby tree, the bird observed as the light of a fire flickered inside the hut and the two monks conversed through the night, their voices rising and falling.

'What is this thing we call time?' asked one monk.

'Time and love are one,' the other monk replied. 'Time is stilled in eternity, where love and your beloved are one.'

'What does that mean?'

'Each flower. Each plant. Each blade of grass is one with love. Love is all there is.'

'So, we should also be love?'

The conversation continued and the bird listened. She was consumed by curiosity. Where had she come from? Was she too made from love? What about the tree that was her home? Did love make that tree?

She then further pondered. What is time? Why does it bring us here, only to take us away again?

The bird picked a nut from the tree. She turned it this way and that. The bird mused that the nut has its own delicious nature, but what of time? How could she understand its essence, find a way to hold it, even for a moment, in her grasp? The bird longed to find a piece of time and lie quietly with it in her nest, to examine it, to understand it. Even if it took months or years, she was willing to wait. If only she could find time, she thought, surely she would find herself as well.

After many days and nights of considering time, the bird collected a small piece of soil from the forest floor. Deep in thought, she studied it, turning it over in her beak, seeking the answers she longed for. She remembered the words of the monk: 'Time is stilled in eternity, where love and your beloved are one. Each flower. Each plant. Each blade of grass is one with love. Love is all there is,' he had said.

But the bird could not find the truth in his words. The clod of earth from forest floor revealed nothing to her. Where was love, if time was hidden within it? She recalled the waterfalls, endlessly tumbling in the north of the forest, and imagined herself as a part of them. She remembered the days spent listening to the sound of the water, the constant, soothing rush. She imagined herself as the waterfall itself, her form dissolving into the water, her spirit becoming the endless stream of life.

Then, one noon, while soaring above the forest, the bird noticed something was amiss. The monk's hut, which had always stood on the side of the forest, was gone. In its place, only a pile of ashes remained, smouldering in the daylight. The hut had been ravaged by fire and was now reduced to cinders. Then she noticed flames from the forest too. The flames had started at the edge of the forest but were now licking hungrily and spreading quickly. She raced to her ancient tree home and saw that the fire was getting closer and closer to the great tree.

She flapped her wings feverishly, hoping to extinguish the flames. But it was futile, the fire raged on, growing stronger with every passing moment.

In a final act of desperation, the bird flew to the spring, dipping her wings in the cool water, and raced back to the tree, shaking the droplets over the flames. But it was not enough. The water droplets sizzled into steam the moment they touched the fire, evaporating into the heat. Despair gripped the bird's heart as she realised that the fire was relentless, devouring the ancient tree that had stood for millennia. As the flames engulfed the great tree, the bird's heart broke. Why was there no rain to save the tree? Why did the downpours that nourished the forest not come here, now, in their hour of need?

In her grief and desperation, the bird let out a piercing cry. A cry that was at once tragic and passionate. A cry that echoed through the burning forest. In that moment, the bird could see the image of the monk, the sun behind the mountain peak and the endless rush of the waterfall to the north. Each was a symbol of eternity and the cycle of life. She felt love pour through her heart and without hesitation, the bird plunged into the flames. She did not fear the fire; instead, she embraced it.

The next morning, the forest was eerily calm. The sun's rays pierced through the lingering smoke, but there was no symphony of birds, no sound of life. The fire had reduced much of the forest to ash, the great tree still standing but with most of its branches charred and lifeless. The once-thriving sanctuary was now a graveyard of silence.

The animals that had survived called out to one another, their voices tinged with sorrow. The great golden bird, born from a golden egg, had saved them all and had put out the fire. She had become one with the flames and had been reduced to ash. Her act was one of selfless love. She had become love.

But the bird would return. From the ashes she would be reborn again as the golden bird. The cycle of her life would go onwards and ever more through time. Time interwoven with love.

The phoenix serves as a powerful metaphor for the human experience of facing challenges, experiencing loss and rising again with renewed strength and hope. Just as the phoenix is reborn in fire, we are reborn through learning and understanding.

24

Clever Gretel

This Brothers Grimm tale was first published in 1819. It focuses on a greedy yet crafty character named Gretel. The Grimms obtained the tale from Andreas Strobl's collection of tales but in his original version Gretel is caught and ends up living a miserable life after her master throws her out. This version is more similar to the Grimm narrative.

Once upon a time, there was a cook named Gretel who took great pride in her appearance. She wore red-heeled shoes and whenever she stepped out in them, she would walk with a cheerful sway, thinking to herself, 'You are a beautiful girl!' This self-admiration often put her in such high spirits that upon returning home, she would indulge in a drink of wine. The wine would stir her appetite, leading her to sample the finest dishes she had prepared, all the while justifying it by saying, 'The cook must know how the food tastes.'

One day, Gretel's master approached her with a request. 'Gretel,' he said. 'We have a guest coming this evening. Prepare two chickens for the meal and make sure they are cooked to perfection.'

'Yes, indeed, sir,' Gretel replied enthusiastically.

She got to work immediately. She killed the chickens and plucked them. She then skewered them, seasoned them and began to roast them. They browned beautifully and soon filled the kitchen with a mouth-watering aroma. But as the chickens neared perfection, the guest had still not arrived.

'Master,' called Gretel. 'If the guest doesn't come soon, I'll have to take the chickens off the fire. It would be a shame if they aren't eaten at their best.'

'You're right,' her master agreed. 'I'll go and fetch the guest myself.'

With the master gone, Gretel set the spit with the chickens aside. Feeling the heat from the fire had made her thirsty, so she decided to run down to the cellar for a quick drink.

'God bless it for you, Gretel!' she toasted herself, taking a hearty gulp from the jug. Returning to the kitchen, Gretel placed the chickens back over the fire, basted them with butter and continued to turn the spit. The delicious smell was irresistible.

'I should make sure they're perfect,' she thought, tasting a piece with her fingers. 'Oh, these chickens are divine! It would be a sin not to eat them while they're hot and juicy.'

Gretel glanced out the window, hoping to see her master and his guest. Seeing no one, she turned back to the fire. Noticing that one wing was starting to burn, she decided to cut it off and eat it. It was so delicious that she couldn't help herself and ate the other wing as well. Once more, she looked out the window, but still saw no sign of the master or his guest.

'Perhaps they've decided to dine elsewhere,' Gretel said out loud. 'Well, Gretel, don't let good food go to waste! You might as well enjoy it.'

She ran down to the cellar for another drink, savouring the wine, and then polished off the first chicken. With one chicken gone and the master still not back, Gretel eyed the second chicken.

'Where one goes, the other should follow. They're a pair. What's right for one can't be wrong for the other.'

Convincing herself, she took another drink and proceeded to devour the second chicken.

As she was finishing the last bite, the master returned, calling out, 'Gretel, hurry up, the guest is right behind me!'

'Yes, sir, I'm just getting everything ready,' Gretel answered quickly.

The master, seeing the table set, picked up a large knife to carve the chickens and stood in the hallway, sharpening it. Just then, the guest arrived and knocked politely at the door. Gretel hurried over, but when she saw the guest she put a finger to her lips and whispered urgently, 'Be quiet! Leave now, quickly! If my master catches you, you'll regret it. Yes, he invited you for dinner, but what he really wants is to cut off both of your ears. Listen! He's sharpening his knife right now for it.'

The guest heard the knife sharpening and, terrified, fled down the steps as fast as he could.

Gretel, not one to waste an opportunity, rushed to her master, crying out, 'What kind of guest did you invite?'

'Why, Gretel? What happened?' her master asked, confused.

'Just as I was about to bring the chickens out, he grabbed them both and ran off!'

'Well, I never! How rude!' the master exclaimed, lamenting the loss of the delicious meal. 'He could have at least left one chicken for me!'

He called out to the fleeing guest, 'Stop! Just one! Just one!'

Knife still in hand, he chased after him. The terrified guest held on to his ears and ran even faster. Fortunately, he got home with both ears intact.

As for the master, he had to settle for soup. While Gretel's belly was bursting from both tasty chickens.

Clever Gretel

Gretel's 'just one more' attitude is something we can all feel sometimes. Just one more chocolate, just one more glass of wine. It seems like a good idea but then we regret it afterwards. An extreme example of this is the fictional character of Mr Creosote from the Monty Python movie The Meaning of Life. *He is a monstrously greedy customer in a restaurant who eats a revolting amount of food. He ends up eating a final 'wafer-thin mint' and explodes. While this might be hyperbole, there are times when we all need to be more disciplined.*

The Wyrm, the Eagle and the Beetle

In October 2018, the UK government became the first in the world to publish a loneliness reduction strategy and, following this, appointed a new ministerial role: that of a Minister for Loneliness. Loneliness, as mentioned earlier in this book, is a real threat to our health and wellbeing. The following tale tells of a lonely boy who finds companionship. This companionship begins with one random act of kindness.

Askelad sat by his father's side. He knew that the old man was dying but wanted to make the old man's passing as comfortable as he could. Askelad bathed his father's brow, gave him sips of water from the stream and told him stories.

Before the old man died, he gave his only son the only thing he had to give: his sword and kind words. 'Askelad, I give you my sword. I ask you to always be honest and listen to your heart. Be kind as often as you can.'

With those words said, the old man died. Askelad wept. He was all alone. He then picked up the rusted, brittle sword, packed some bread and set off to find his way in the world.

He wandered for many days and long nights. He felt as lonely as an echo in a canyon.

One day, as he walked, he heard a terrible commotion coming from over the other side of a rocky hill. Askelad climbed to the top. Looking down he saw a huge legless dragon, known as a wyrm. Askelad might have had his father's old sword but he did not want to fight against such a ferocious creature. He turned to walk in the other direction. But the wyrm roared words directly at Askelad. 'Can you come down here and help us?'

Askelad paused. This was foolishness. He needed to be far away and fast. What could he do to help a wyrm? He would surely be devoured!

Yet, Askelad found himself scaling down the hill towards the legless dragon. He saw that the wyrm was with two other animals. There was a great eagle and a tiny beetle. The three unlikely companions stood together with woeful expressions. Askelad realised that the eagle was caught in a snare.

'If I try to free my friend, I'm more likely to remove her leg,' the wyrm explained. 'Our other friend has tried but cannot do it. Will you release the snare?'

Askelad carefully pulled free the metal loop and the eagle flapped her wings vigorously. Then the boy drew his father's sword and sliced the metal snare in two so that it could not catch any other animal. But, as he did, the rusted old sword broke in two. He felt sad for breaking his father's sword but decided not to mention it and instead said, 'Can I help you with anything else?'

'No but thank you, my friend,' the wyrm replied.

The wyrm, eagle and beetle talked to Askelad for the rest of the day, telling their stories and singing songs.

'Did you snap your sword while untying me?' asked the eagle after a while.

'Indeed I did, my friend,' said Askelad sadly. 'But no matter.'

'I think we owe our new friend a gift in return for his kindness,' the eagle said to the wyrm. 'Do you agree?'

The beetle hopped from one leg to another excitedly.

'I certainly do!'

The wyrm took in a long, deep breath and then let out a blast of hot, steamy breath over Askelad. It shocked the boy at first but didn't hurt. He felt warm and tingled all over.

'What did you do?' he asked.

'I've given you the power to transmogrify into a wyrm, an eagle or a beetle any time you like.'

With that the three companions set off, thanking Askelad for his help and his companionship. The boy climbed back up to the top of the hill. As he climbed, he decided to try out his new power straight away. Why climb when he could fly? Askelad closed his eyes and imagined himself an eagle. And he was! Askelad the eagle soared into the air and flew above the hills and mountains for many miles.

Eventually, he grew tired, so he landed in a tree next to a large palace. Suddenly he was grabbed and stuffed into a golden cage. The princess of the palace had seen Askelad the eagle land and thought he would make a beautiful pet. She took him to her bedroom and placed him on a table. She then rushed off to the kitchen to get some cuts of meat to feed to her new bird.

Askelad imagined himself a beetle. And he was! Askelad the beetle then walked out of the cage and turned back into a boy. When the princess returned she was astonished.

'Who are you? What are you doing in my bedroom? Where's my new pet?' she demanded.

'My name is Askelad,' beamed the boy. 'It's nice to meet you.'

'GET OUT!' she screamed.

Askelad climbed on to the windowsill, imagined himself an eagle and flew off. He circled the palace a few times but as he was about to fly away, a huge giant came stomping across the land. Askelad the eagle landed in that same tree again and watched what would happen next.

The king's guards emerged from the palace shooting arrows and waving swords, but they were all swept aside by the monstrous giant. It punched a hole through the palace walls, reached inside, grabbed the princess and set off with her. His massive fingers encircled her entirely but Askelad could still hear her screaming.

The king ran out of the palace, calling after his daughter, but eventually sank down to his knees and wept in despair.

Askelad imagined himself a boy and leapt down from the tree.

'Don't worry!' he said. 'I'll save your daughter!'

The king looked at the boy through his tears and simply shook his head. Askelad became an eagle and flew off in pursuit of the giant and the princess. It was easy to follow such an enormous beast. Each footstep made a thundering booming sound and left a mighty imprint upon the earth.

The giant arrived at a gigantic cave. It stepped into the darkness, then rolled a huge boulder across the entrance to stop anyone else from entering. Askelad the eagle landed on the ground, imagined himself a beetle then crawled in through a tiny gap.

Once inside, Askelad the beetle saw the giant was building a fire and had set a large cauldron over the top filled with water. It then looked at the princess in its massive hand and smiled a toothy, slavering grin.

Askelad the beetle imagined himself a wyrm and roared with fury. The giant was so surprised that he dropped the princess but Askelad the wyrm caught her with his tail and set her down gently. The giant landed a punch on Askelad the wyrm's head and he was knocked to the other side of the cave.

A ferocious battle then ensued.

The giant punched, kicked, butted, bit and scratched. Askelad the wyrm ducked, weaved, rolled, coiled and uncoiled until he saw his chance. With his long teeth he lunged and ripped out the giant's throat. Blood sprayed the walls of the cave and the giant fell down as a lifeless corpse. Askelad the wyrm then used his mighty strength to push aside the boulder blocking the exit. He then imagined himself a boy and turned to face the princess.

They walked back to her palace. It had only taken the giant and Askelad the eagle moments to travel the great distance from palace to giant's cave, but the walk was much longer.

The princess and Askelad the boy took their time. They enjoyed each other's company. They talked about this and that, what was and what wasn't.

Askelad was invited to stay at the palace for as long as he wanted. He accepted the offer and spent each day with the princess. The pair had found love and Askelad was to be lonely no longer.

Kindness is something that we can all seek to do more of. Kindness could be something as simple as smiling at someone, holding a door open or giving a compliment. Practising kindness improves your mental wellbeing. Acts of kindness have been linked to increased levels of happiness, satisfaction and overall wellbeing. Engaging in kind actions can reduce stress, anxiety, and symptoms of depression. It might not lead us to super powers, like Askelad, but it can help us feel so much better.

26

The Gossip

Gossiping is largely considered to be something rather negative. Despite this, in a 1997 study, it was estimated that in two thirds of our conversations people are talking about others who are not present. We engage in gossip to bond with our colleagues, entertain others, to exchange information, to vent emotions and to maintain social order.

Some researchers argue that gossip helped our ancestors survive. Evolutionary psychologist Robin Dunbar first pioneered this idea, comparing gossip to the grooming primates engage in as a means of bonding. Dunbar goes on to say that gossiping gives humans the ability to spread valuable information to very large social networks.

In this Russian folk tale we see how a wife deals with her husband's constant gossiping.

Once upon a time, there was an elderly couple who lived at the edge of a dense forest. They resided on land owned by a wealthy landlord, who thought only of his own needs. Every month, he collected rent, increasing the amount by a single coin each time.

One day, after months of escalating demands, the old woman turned to her husband in despair.

'How are we going to pay this month's rent? If we don't have the money, the landlord will evict us!'

'It'll be fine,' the old man replied nonchalantly and headed off to the pub to meet his friends.

Worried and anxious, the old woman paced their modest home, unable to shake her growing dread. She decided to take a walk to soothe her nerves. With a heavy heart, she set out into the forest.

As she wandered, she came across an overturned tree. She sat down, contemplating their dire situation, when she noticed a nearby tree that was starkly different from the others. It was barren, devoid of leaves and appeared to be withering, unlike the lush greenery around it.

Curiosity piqued, she began to dig around the roots of the struggling tree. Her fingers soon struck something hard and smooth. Digging further, she uncovered a large clay pot with a wooden lid. She pulled with all her might and fell backward, clutching the pot.

'This must be what's stunting the tree's growth,' she murmured to herself.

Opening the pot, she gasped at the sight of gold coins brimming inside.

'My goodness!' she exclaimed, elated.

The old woman jumped up and hugged the barren tree in joy.

'Thank you, my friend! Your struggle has led me to this treasure. I hope this will help us both thrive.'

With a newfound spring in her step, she began walking back home. But a troubling thought crept into her mind ... her husband.

He could never keep a secret, especially after a few drinks with his friends. If the landlord learned about the treasure found on his property, he would surely claim it for himself.

The old woman paused and pondered deeply. Then, she smiled to herself.

She returned to the tree and reburied the pot of gold, whispering, 'Don't worry, I'll come back for you later.'

Rushing home, she gathered six eggs, four rashers of bacon and a chicken leg. She placed these in a basket before heading back into the forest. She carefully piled the eggs at the base of one tree, draped the bacon over the branches of another and wedged the chicken leg into a hollow trunk near the barren tree.

Just as she finished, her husband returned from the pub.

'Husband!' she cried with excitement. 'I've found magical trees in the forest!'

'Magical trees? Have you lost your mind?' he laughed incredulously.

'It's true!' she beamed. 'One tree lays eggs, another grows bacon, a third produces chicken legs, and the fourth … yields gold from its roots! I've seen it all!'

'Prove it!' he challenged, still sceptical.

She led him through the forest, showing him the trees with the eggs, bacon and chicken leg. Finally, they reached the barren tree. She unearthed the pot of gold and her husband was stunned into silence.

'We must keep this hidden under the tree,' she cautioned. 'If the landlord discovers it, he'll take it all. This must remain our secret.'

Her husband nodded, and they returned home, jubilant and relieved. But the next day, the old man began to grumble.

'What good is all that gold if we can't spend it? Why not keep it in our house?'

'If the landlord learns we have money, he'll search the house and seize it,' she replied firmly.

The old man sighed in frustration. 'Can't I just take a few coins to the pub? I promise I won't tell anyone.'

Anticipating his request, the old woman reluctantly agreed. 'Alright, but only two coins. We can't risk losing it all.'

She handed him two coins and he eagerly rushed to the pub. Soon, the ale had loosened his tongue and he began buying rounds for everyone as he boasted about his newfound wealth.

The next morning, the landlord pounded on their door. The old woman greeted him calmly.

'Your husband was bragging last night about finding gold on my land,' the landlord bellowed. 'Show me the gold or you'll be evicted!'

The old man, sheepish and hungover, led the landlord into the forest. After a fruitless search, the furious landlord stormed back, bursting into their home.

'Your husband is a fool! He took me on a wild chase, babbling about trees that lay eggs and grow bacon, only to show me a barren tree with no gold. I should have known better than to listen to pub gossip!'

With a final curse, he left, leaving the couple in peace.

'I'm sorry,' the old man mumbled. 'From now on, I'll leave our money to you.'

They laughed heartily. The old woman, having anticipated the outcome, had already moved the pot of gold to a hidden spot in their garden. They only dug up coins when they needed them and the old couple lived happily in their home for the rest of their days, free from the landlord's tyranny.

If we were asked if we often gossip then we would probably deny it. Is this because gossip doesn't sit well on our conscience?

Before we engage in gossiping, perhaps we should ask ourselves these three questions:

1. How does passing this information help you or another person?
2. Are you sharing this information out of envy?
3. Are you sharing the information out of enmity?

27

Three Eyes, Two Eyes and One Eye

This folk tale is from Jacob and Wilhelm Grimm's book Children's and Household Tales *from 1812. I've changed a few things around, as happens in any retelling, but the storyline is the same. There are acts of kindness here, a theme throughout this book, but it is what happens at the end of the story that is worth pondering upon.*

Once upon a time, there was an old woman who had three eyes. She had two daughters. The eldest had one eye and her youngest had two eyes.

Three Eyes and One Eye used to treat Two Eyes terribly. They made her do all the cooking and cleaning. They made her sleep on the floor in the kitchen. They wouldn't give her any food except for the scraps from their plates. The only thing that gave Two Eyes comfort was her pet goat that she kept in a pen in the garden.

One day, Two Eyes was taking her goat for a walk through the woods when her hunger became too much to bear and she burst into tears. Just then, an old woman came shuffling through the woods. She wore a large cloak that engulfed her entirely.

'What's the matter with you, dear girl?' asked the old woman.

'It's my mother and sister,' sniffed Two Eyes. 'They don't give me anything to eat and they treat me like a slave.'

'Oh dear,' said the old woman. 'Don't worry. I can help.'

She pulled a gnarled and twisted stick from beneath her cavernous cloak.

'May I?'

Two Eyes nodded and the old woman crouched down by the goat. She whispered words in a language that Two Eyes had never heard before. The old woman moved the stick rhythmically as she muttered these words.

'This goat now possesses power,' the old woman announced. 'Ask it for any food or drink and it will appear. You will never be hungry again.'

'Oh, thank you!' beamed Two Eyes.

'Just say, "Little goat, bleat. Little table, appear," and you will have all the food you would ever need,' the old woman said then shuffled off into the woods.

Two Eyes looked at her goat and said, 'Little goat, bleat. Little table, appear.'

The goat immediately opened its mouth wide and out fell a table. On it was a steaming hot loaf of freshly baked bread and a small wheel of cheese. Both of the girl's eyes were round with amazement.

Two Eyes ate until her belly was bursting.

The next day, after she had done her work, Two Eyes took the goat back into the woods. 'Little goat, bleat. Little table, appear.'

The table was produced with a steaming bowl of broth on it and Two Eyes hungrily devoured the lot.

Two Eyes went to sleep that night with a full belly and a smile on her face. But, Three Eyes noticed that her youngest daughter didn't want the scraps from her plate any more.

'Tomorrow,' Three Eyes said to One Eye, 'we'll follow that sister of yours and find out where she's getting her food from.'

The following morning, Three Eyes and One Eye followed Two Eyes into the woods. They hid behind a large tree, watching and listening as Two Eyes spoke to the goat: 'Little goat, bleat. Little table, appear.'

The table was produced, a hot bowl of soup sat steaming upon it and Two Eyes began to eat.

Three Eyes raced from behind the tree.

'The beast is cursed!' she screeched and took a knife from her dress.

She slit the goat's throat and wiped the blade clean on Two Eyes' dress.

'You were bringing a cursed goat to our home! Shame on you!'

Three Eyes and One Eye then went back to the house, leaving Two Eyes sobbing over the body of the goat.

Just then, the old woman came walking through the woods again.

'What happened to the magic goat, dear girl?' asked the old woman.

'My mother killed him!' wailed Two Eyes.

'Oh dear,' said the old woman. 'But don't worry. I can help.'

She pulled the gnarled and twisted stick from her cloak. She repeated the rhythmic movements from before and muttered more strange words.

When she had finished, the old woman said, 'Bury the goat in your garden and see what happens in the morning.'

Two Eyes thanked the old woman and carried the dead goat back to her home. When she arrived, she buried the body in the garden.

Two Eyes slept on the kitchen floor, then in the morning she drew the curtains and gasped. Where the goat had been buried there now stood a beautiful silver tree with bronze leaves and golden apples.

Two Eyes stepped outside and gazed at the tree. She was soon joined by Three Eyes and One Eye, who were also amazed. Suddenly they heard a chinking and a clunking as a knight rode past their house. He stopped when he saw the tree and removed his helmet.

'Whoever picks one of those golden apples for me will be rewarded greatly.'

Three Eyes immediately raced over and tried to climb the tree, but the silver bark was too smooth and she could not do it. One Eye leapt up into the air trying to grab an apple. But the branches were too high and she couldn't do it either. Two Eyes stepped forward and the tree bowed to her. It dropped a golden apple into her hand.

She gave it to the knight, who said, 'Thank you! You can claim your reward at my castle.'

He helped Two Eyes to climb up on to the horse and they trotted away.

'Oh well,' sneered Three Eyes. 'We don't need her. We'll take an axe, chop down the tree and be rich.'

These words were only just spoken when the tree lifted up its roots from the ground and walked off after Two Eyes and the knight. It arrived at the castle of the knight, then plunged its roots into the ground.

The reward Two Eyes was given was to live a life of luxury and leisure in the castle as a Lady of the Land. She spent many happy months there until one day there was a banging at the castle gates. Two bedraggled and starving women stood there begging for food. One had three eyes and the other had one eye. Without Two Eyes to look after them, Three Eyes and One Eye had to travel the land begging for food.

When Two Eyes saw her mother and sister begging for food, did she turn them away? Of course not, she invited them inside and gave them a feast. Three Eyes and One Eye saw how unfair they had been to Two Eyes. They begged for forgiveness.

Two Eyes not only forgave them but also invited them both to live with her in the castle.

'Forgiving a person who has wronged you is never easy, but dwelling on those events and reliving them over and over can fill your mind with negative thoughts and suppressed anger,' says Dr Tyler VanderWeele, co-director of the Initiative on Health, Religion, and Spirituality at the Harvard T.H. Chan School of Public Health. 'Yet, when you learn to forgive, you are no longer trapped by the past actions of others and can finally feel free.'

The power of forgiveness is real. It can lead you feel empathy and compassion for those who have previously hurt you. This doesn't mean that you forget or excuse past action or harm that has been done to you. It means that it leads to a better understanding of other people and why they do the things that they do.

28

Princess Rat

Wisdom enables us to be effective decision-makers, improves our interpersonal relationships and helps us to resolve conflicts. But in this tale there is a princess who uses her wisdom to get exactly what she wants.

Once there lived a king and queen. They had so much money that their roof tiles were made from glowing gold. So much money that their windows were made from beautiful diamonds. So much money that their palace walls were made from shining silver. But this money did not make them happy. The couple longed for children. They had wanted children for such a long time that they eventually sent for the most powerful wizard in the whole of the land to help them.

'Wizard,' boomed the king. 'Can you give us children?'

The wizard bowed low. The wizard stepped towards the king. The wizard spoke.

'No,' he said. 'But … I would suggest that you get yourself a pet. Pets can be an excellent substitute for children!'

The king and queen thought about this for some time, then finally agreed. But what pet would be suitable? The royal pair decided to visit the town where there was a pet shop. There, they saw puppies and kittens. But they also saw something they made them both beam great smiles … a rat. A tiny brown rat with a pink twitching nose.

'Perfect!' they both exclaimed.

The rat was taken to the palace and given a large purple cushion to sit upon. That rat was given everything she could ever want. She ate only the finest cheese and drank only the sweetest milk. She grew into a beautiful brown rat and the king and queen were delighted with her.

One day, the king was watching the queen play with the rat. He sighed and said, 'Wouldn't it be wonderful if she were a *real* princess. A *human* princess instead of a rat princess.'

'Well get that wizard back here then,' suggested the queen.

The wizard was summoned before the king once again.

'Wizard,' boomed the king. 'Can you turn our beautiful rat into a princess?'

The wizard bowed low. The wizard stepped towards the king. The wizard spoke.

'Yes,' he said. 'But … if I do this for you it will use up all of my magic. I will never be able to perform any other magical tasks ever again. Are you quite certain this is what you want?'

'I am!' answered the king.

'If I do this,' continued the wizard, 'she will still be a rat on the inside even though she will look like a human on the outside.'

'I don't care, do it!' smiled the king.

'Are you sure?' asked the wizard.

'We are positive!' beamed the king.

The wizard bowed, then produced a gnarled and twisted wand from his long, blue cloak. He pointed the wand at the rat. The wizard muttered strange magical words and there was a flash of golden light.

There wasn't a rat there anymore. Now, there was a princess. A princess with long brown hair and a pink, twitching nose. The princess opened her mouth and spoke.

'Have you got any cheese?'

The king, queen and princess lived together happily in the palace for many years, but one day the king was watching the queen play with the princess.

He sighed and said, 'It's all very well playing games but I think it's about time the princess was married.'

'But who will I marry?' asked the princess while twitching her pink nose.

'Hmm,' thought the king. 'I'd say he'd have to be very powerful. The most powerful man in the world.'

The king rubbed his grey beard thoughtfully and walked over to his diamond window. He looked at the world outside. His eyes were blinded by the powerful sun.

Then suddenly he said, 'The sun! The sun is the most powerful of all. You shall marry the sun.'

'The sun?' giggled the princess. 'I don't want to marry the sun. Anyway, the sun isn't the most powerful because all it takes is a cloud to move in front of the sun and the sun loses its power. Clouds are much more powerful than the sun.'

'A cloud!' called the king. 'You shall marry a cloud.'

'A cloud?' laughed the princess. 'I don't want to marry a cloud. All it takes is a gust of wind and that cloud would be blown away. The wind is much more powerful than a cloud.'

'The wind!' shouted the king, 'You shall marry the wind.'

'The wind?' chortled the princess, 'I don't want to marry the wind. The wind could blow all day but it couldn't blow down a mountain. A mountain is much more powerful than the wind.'

'A mountain!' boomed the king. 'You shall marry a mountain.'

'A mountain?' chuckled the princess. 'I don't want to marry a mountain! All it would take is a handsome young rat and he could chew his way right through a mountain. A rat is much more powerful than a mountain.'

'A rat!' roared the king. 'You shall marry a rat.'

'Alright then,' smiled the princess, 'I will.'

A whole mischief of rats were brought to the palace. The princess sat and talked to each one in turn for days on end. Eventually, the princess announced that she had found the perfect match. A handsome brown rat was the one for her.

The king looked at the princess and the rat together. He sighed and said, 'This doesn't seem right. I'd much prefer it if he were a prince or a human at least.'

'Well get that wizard back here then,' suggested the queen.

The wizard was summoned before the king once more.

'Wizard,' boomed the king. 'Can you turn that rat into a prince?'

The wizard bowed low. The wizard stepped towards the king. The wizard spoke.

'No,' he said. 'I told you that once the princess was turned from rat into human all of my magic would be used up. But … I have heard stories about princesses kissing frogs, then the frogs turn into princes. Perhaps this will be the same if a princess kisses a rat.'

'Very well, they shall kiss. But I don't want them kissing until they are married.'

The wedding was organised immediately. The palace was decorated and guests were invited. As soon as all was ready the princess and the rat were married. The princess then picked up the rat and kissed him on his pink nose.

There was a flash of golden light and there wasn't a rat there anymore. Now, there were two rats. The princess had been turned back into a rat.

The rats were the prince and princess of the land for many years until eventually they became the king and queen themselves. Those two rats ruled more wisely than any humans had ever done before.

The Italian philosopher, diplomat and author Niccolo Machiavelli said, 'Before all else, be armed.' The princess in this tale knew how to persuade her father to let her marry a rat. She knew that if she just asked outright then she would be turned down. Her approach was more Machiavellian. She armed herself with wisdom. When we ask for things that we might want, such as a job promotion, then we would be wise to be armed with the right questions and appropriate knowledge before we rush in. Arm yourself with wisdom in every situation.

29

The Hunger

We all want things that we cannot have. This strange story tells of a man who covets something so much that he risks everything to get it. But angering Roman gods is not the best idea, as we shall see here …

Outside the gates of Rome there was a forest of sacred oak trees. No one was allowed to cut down these trees as they belonged to Ceres, the goddess of harvests.

Erysichthon had been walking through a path in the forest. Shimmering sunlight descended here and there, decorating the labyrinth of branches with golden patches. Tangled trees clawed the air as he trudged past. Curling creepers were wrapped around every tree. There was a heavy scent of bark and detritus. Occasionally the sound of a woodpecker could be heard, but apart from this it was eerily quiet.

As he walked away from the path the air became cooler and he was shrouded in shade. The forest was filled with knotted and crooked trees here as he slowly disappeared into the gloom. Here, darkness had descended upon the ferns and trees. It was summer but the season felt like a memory now. Patches of sunlight broke through the trees above and parts of trees shone in the dim light. Tawny brown bark was everywhere. As Erysichthon walked, he felt spiderweb strands stroke his skin.

Then he saw them. He stopped. Anticipation fizzed in the air. The seconds trickled by ever so slowly. He waited and waited. Then moved towards them and stroked their bark. The sacred trees of Ceres were unmistakable. They were towering, magnificent and worth money.

The woodcutter pulled his axe from its leather case. His eyes darted this way and that. He held the axe at its head and cut at a tree. The iron cut through the bark easily.

Then he waited.

Nothing happened. No wrath from above. Nothing. He waited a few moments more and thought of the money he would make.

Then he began to swing his axe. Erysichthon thought of his daughter, Melia. She would be proud of her father. He would have money. They would eat well.

The trees oozed sap. They looked like tears but that was nonsense. It was just sap. Trees don't cry.

The woodcutter filled his wooden barrow and wheeled it back to the path. He loaded the wood on to a cart next to his tethered horse. He returned to the sacred oaks and chopped down another.

He sold the wood and waited for any repercussions from on high. When there were none, he returned to the sacred forest the next day. And the next.

Ceres returned to her forest after bringing fruit to the orchards across the Roman Empire. When she saw her forest had been reduced to stumps she raised her arms to the sky and said, 'Only an empty, hollow man could do such a thing.'

Erysichthon was strolling back through the Roman markets having sold all of his wood for many a coin.

'All of that work has made me hungry,' he said to himself, and he bought some bacon and some smoked fish.

After he had eaten these, he was still hungry, so he bought a whole side of venison.

But even after this was consumed, he was *still* hungry, so he bought cheese, bread, duck, chicken and goose. But even after he had spent all of his money and eaten everything, the hunger would just not go away.

Erysichthon ran home, collected everything he could carry and began to sell his possessions. With the money he bought a whole ox and every fish the fisherman had caught that day. But it was no good. The hunger gripped him even more tightly and now he had nothing left to sell.

'We have nothing left. Pray to the gods to take your terrible hunger away!' cried his daughter, Melia.

But Erysichthon smiled and said, 'I hear a young slave girl gets a good price!'

He grabbed his daughter. Melia kicked and screamed but Erysichthon would not listen to her cries. He simply carried her under his strong arms off to the slave market to sell.

Melia managed to struggle free from her father's iron grip and ran out of the city gates, then down to the riverbank. Her father chased her but he was so overcome by hunger that he stopped when he saw a freshwater crab scuttle along the mud in front of him. Erysichthon thought how delicious the crab looked and grabbed it. The crab kicked its legs as Erysichthon stuffed it into his mouth. There was a terrible crunching sound as he chewed away. Swallowing bits of shell and claw, Erysichthon winced at each bite but continued the horrible feast.

When he had finished, Erysichthon realised he was alone on the riverbank. He wiped away the last of the shell from his mouth with the back of his hand. He tasted the salty tang of his sweat and could not resist taking a small bite. It hurt. He yelped with pain but then he took another and another and another.

Meanwhile, Melia had run back to the market for help. She found one of her father's friends and explained to him what had happened. She led the friend to the beach but it was too late. Eriscython's lifeless body was there on the riverbank. He was covered in bites of his own making and had bled out on to the mud. Ceres had taken her revenge on the empty, hollow man who had cut down her trees.

Alice Binder from the University of Vienna says that 'anything which seems to be unavailable is, as a result, more desirable'. In other words, we want things even more when we are told we cannot have them. In psychology this is known as the 'Forbidden Fruit Effect'. But not getting what we want is profoundly good for us. The Dalai Lama says, 'Remember that sometimes not getting what you want is a wonderful stroke of luck.' When we push ourselves through times when we are disappointed, we can find ourselves on the other side wiser and stronger. By working through difficult times in life, we grow into better selves.

30

Raven and the First Humans

Native Americans decorated totem poles with carvings of Raven at the top to remind them that the creator bird was watching them from above. This tale tells of the creation of the Earth and warns us of the repercussions of not looking after our precious home.

Raven lived in the midnight sky of space and lived alone. He was a giant, black bird, but when he pushed his beak on top of his head, Raven would become a winged man. There was great magic in Raven's wings. He would flap them and he could make anything he imagined.

Raven grew tired of living in the darkness of space, so he flapped his wings four times and the great magic was released. The sun appeared in space. It filled Raven with warmth and light. Now light shone constantly in the darkness.

Then Raven grew tired of flying, so he flapped his wings four times and the Earth appeared. Raven flew down to Earth and pushed his beak on top of his head. Then he walked around the Earth but it wobbled like jelly. Raven flapped his wings four times and this great magic made the mountains and the ground.

Raven thought the Earth was dull so he thought and he imagined. Then he flapped his wings and on the fourth time there was the sea, the rivers, the lakes, the ponds.

But still Raven imagined more. He flapped his wings four times and made the trees, the flowers, the bushes, the grasses, the shrubs, the ferns … all plants … including the pea pod plant.

Then Raven was happy. He pushed his beak forward and flew into the sky to enjoy his new view.

Raven came down to the Earth often and enjoyed what he had created. The plants grew and became more beautiful each time Raven saw them.

One day, the pea pod plant popped open. There was a thud and on to the ground landed a man. The first man. Man stood up and looked around. He then began to walk around this new place and smiled at its beauty.

Eventually Raven came visiting. He pushed his beak to the top of his head as he saw the man and spoke. 'Who are you?' asked Raven. 'I didn't make you.'

'I came out of the pea pod plant,' said the man.

'Well, I suppose I did make you then!' laughed Raven.

Man laughed too, but he wasn't sure why. Raven taught the man how to drink from the river and how to eat the fruit of the plants. Man was happy. But as time passed man complained that he was lonely. Raven lived in the vastness of space and only visited the man occasionally; he wanted some company.

So, Raven flapped his wings four times and the great magic created woman. Raven taught the man and the woman how to build a shelter, then left them to get to know each other.

The next time Raven came to visit, man and woman complained that they were hungry. The food from the plants was not enough. Raven flapped his wings and made fishes, deer, cattle, chickens, goats, pigs … all of the animals. Then Raven taught man and woman how to hunt, how to make fire and how to cook the meat.

Raven kept watching man and woman … but from the sky. He watched their children playing and watched them grow up.

He watched their children's children. And their children too. He watched how men and woman flourished on the Earth.

But men and women became greedy. They took too much from Earth. They took more than they needed. They threw away what they didn't use. They wasted what Raven had given them.

So, Raven took away the sun. Now it was no longer day all of the time. It was darkness. It was an eternal night. Men and women were sorry. They called out to Raven to give them back the sun, give them back the light.

Raven felt sorry for men and women. He gave them back the sun. But only for half of the time. Raven made day and night. During the day the sun shone. During the night Raven kept the sun hidden. This was to remind men and women not to be greedy. The day time was for hunting and the night time was for resting.

Raven then flapped his wings four times again and with this strong magic he made lots of smaller ravens. These he sent down to Earth to watch the humans. If they were too greedy again then these ravens would fly into the sky and tell Raven. Then the sun would be taken away from men and women forever.

We know that the way the global economy manages natural resources deeply influences the Earth's climate. Now more than ever, we need to cherish the plants and animals of our world. We need to more efficient and use less energy. Perhaps Raven can teach us a better way of living even today.

31

The Tree of Knowledge

Academic learning and logical thinking can lead to a growth in intelligence, but wisdom comes from the use of judgement before action that is usually derived from life experience. Moral dilemmas are a good testing place for applying wisdom in one's life. The following tale poses the suggestion that wisdom can be found in an object. An object that can make even the most foolish person wise.

Mendel the Fool was begging from village to village, town to town, city to city. What little money he got, he spent on expensive food and wine. He had tried lots of jobs but nobody wanted a fool working for them. One day, Mendel was walking the length of a long, dusty track when suddenly a huge storm raged in the sky.

The wind howled and the rain burst from the clouds. Everything was swept up into the air. Mendel grabbed on to a large rock and held on tight. The wind and the rain swirled all around and Mendel was lifted into the air, but still he kept his grip. Even a fool knows when his life is in danger!

After many minutes had passed the storm disappeared as quickly as it had appeared.

Mendel let go of the rock and rose to his feet. Everything became clear. Not just in the sky but in Mendel's' mind. He understood the way of the world. How it was all intricately balanced. He understood the language of the birds around him. Mendel smiled and, lost in new thoughts, wandered to the nearest town.

In the market place he found a group of wise men deep in debate. Mendel answered the questions they had discussed all day long. He solved riddles that people posed to him. He settled disputes. He solved arguments. The people were amazed. Was this the same Mendel they had seen begging earlier? The same fool who needed help to do up his sandals?

Mendel was given coin after coin for his wisdom. For his ability to mediate and philosophise.

Mendel used his money to find food and shelter in a tavern. He asked for a hot bath to be prepared, for the storm had left him dusty and dirty. Mendel took off his robes and his sandals, and as quickly as he became wise, he suddenly became foolish again. He slipped on a bar of soap and fell head first into the bath. Once clean Mendel put his old robes and dirty sandals back on; he instantly became wise again.

What *wise* Mendel realised was that the source of his wisdom was his clothes. What he didn't realise was that during the storm a leaf from the Tree of Knowledge had blown all the way from the Garden of Eden and wedged itself into one of his sandals. This was source of his wisdom.

Mendel became famous across the land. People travelled for miles to hear his lessons and his ability to debate with anyone.

Eventually, news of Mendel's wisdom reached the king. The king sent his messenger and summoned Mendel to his court.

'Ah, you are wise Mendel,' smiled the king when Mendel arrived. 'My daughter has been struck blind as a result of a fever she caught. All of the doctors in the land have tried to heal her … all have failed.

'Can you, wise Mendel, help my daughter?'

'I will try, Your Majesty,' answered Mendel.

Once Mendel saw the king's daughter he instantly fell in love. She was the most beautiful girl he had ever seen.

Mendel opened her closed eyes and knew at once what to do. He went straight to a fig tree that grew outside the king's palace and collected some of the sap, bark and leaves.

Then Mendel used a pestle and mortar to grind the ingredients into a lotion.

Mendel then rubbed the lotion into the princess's eyes … and she could see!

The king was overjoyed. He made Mendel his chief advisor straight away.

Several months passed. The king ruled more wisely than ever with Mendel at his side. But each day the king questioned Mendel about the source of his knowledge. Each day Mendel would reply with the same answer.

'It's my robes and my sandals, Your Majesty.'

'Those dirty old things?' the king would laugh. 'Those robes of a beggar? Come now Mendel, tell me the truth!'

Each day would be the same until eventually the king relented and said, 'Very well, wise Mendel. I believe you. It is your robes and your sandals that bring you great knowledge. After all, you never change them!

'What price do you ask for me to buy them off you?'

'I don't want to sell them. Sorry, Your Majesty,' Mendel replied.

'How about one bag of gold?!' asked the king.

Each day the king would offer Mendel a new price and each day he would refuse.

'Two bags of gold … Three then! Four! Ten!' the king would say.

'I'm sorry,' is all Mendel would reply.

But one day, the king made Mendel a more interesting offer.

'Very well, Mendel the wise,' said the king. 'I offer you half of my kingdom for your robes and your sandals.'

'I don't want to sell them. Sorry, Your Majesty,' Mendel replied.

The king nodded and said, 'Half my kingdom ... and my daughter's hand in marriage.'

Mendel gasped. 'If she agrees then it would be my honour to marry her!'

The princess agreed, she too loved Mendel from the moment he gave her sight back. He was overjoyed to marry the girl he had loved since the moment he saw her.

Mendel gave up his dusty old robes and dirty sandals and changed into luxurious silk clothes and soft leather shoes. He also changed back into a fool.

The king held the robes and sandals in his hand and grimaced. He couldn't bear to wear them as they were now.

'Go and have these cleaned and washed, then bring them straight back to me!' the king ordered his servants.

The robes were washed and the sandals were cleaned.

When the king wore Mendel's washed robes and cleaned sandals, he felt no different. The leaf from the tree of knowledge had been thrown away. He never did admit to anyone he had given up half his kingdom and his daughter for nothing. So, no one found out the secret.

As for Mendel and the princess? They were married and she ruled their half of the kingdom wisely enough for both of them. Mendel may have been a fool again ... but he was a happy fool.

This Jewish folk tale poses the question: what would we give to become wise? Would we give away our most prized possessions? Would we give away our home? Wisdom comes from experience and not, of course, from the ownership of any object. For the philosopher Aristotle, both the wise contemplative way of life and the intelligent practical way of life can both be chosen and they work in harmony with one another. For Aristotle, a person can choose to live both wisely and intelligently, which leads to living a happy life, but both wisdom and intelligence come through experiencing all that life has to offer us.

32

Tattercoats

The story of Cinderella that is so familiar to us is the French version of the story. However, there are many different Cinderella stories from around the world. She is known as 'Rough Face Girl' in Native American myths, 'Yeh-Shen' in China and 'Nyasha' in Africa. In the UK there is 'Cinderlad' from Ireland, 'Rashin Coatie' from Scotland, 'the Little Sinder Girl' from Wales and 'Tattercoats' from England. It is this English version that is retold here and was originally retold by Joseph Jacobs in his book More English Fairy Tales, *first published in 1894.*

There was once a rich man who lived with his wife and three daughters in a large house near to the royal palace. It was the rich man's birthday and he had invited all of his friends from near and far to his house for a great feast. The rich man was having a wonderful time. He ate lots of food and drank far too much wine. Towards the end of the night he was very drunk. He stood up, wobbling.

'Hic! My daughters! Tell me how much you love me!' he said loudly.

'Well Daddy,' began the eldest daughter, 'I love you more than the whole world!'

'Hic! Lovely!' smiled the rich man.

'Oh Daddy,' said the middle daughter, 'I love you more than life itself!'

'Hic! Marvellous!' beamed the rich man.

'Well,' began the youngest daughter as she looked around the room, 'I love you more than …'

'Hic! More than what?' smiled the rich man.

The youngest daughter noticed how much everyone was enjoying their food. She realised that it was all of the herbs and spices that made the food tasty.

'More than what?' the rich man asked again, quickly becoming impatient.

'More than … more than … food loves herbs and spices!' the youngest daughter said smiling.

'More than food loves herbs and spices!?' the rich man bellowed. '*More than food loves herbs and spices!* I don't think you love me at all! Get out! Get out of my house! Hic!'

The youngest daughter burst into tears and ran off into the night. She was walking and crying, crying and walking for a long time. She was shivering as the night was so cold and all she had on was her party dress. She began to pull weeds up that grew along the path. When she had armfuls of these weeds, she sat down on the soft grass and began plaiting them together. She made a whole coat of weeds. She put the coat on and pulled the hood over her head.

Then made her way further along the path until she reached the palace of the king and queen. She knocked at the door and it was instantly opened by the royal butler.

'Yes?' the butler said. 'What can I do for you?'

'I'm homeless, cold and hungry. I need a place to live. I'll wash, cook, clean, I'll do anything you need me to. Please can I stay here?'

'We always need new servants here. You can work in the kitchens in the basement,' said the butler.

'Thank you so much!' beamed the youngest daughter.

She cooked the most delicious dinners in that palace. Everyone loved the youngest daughter's food. It was all the herbs and spices she used that made them so delicious. She became known as Tattercoats because she never took off her coat made from weeds.

One day, the butler burst into the kitchen.

'There's to be a ball! A feast and a dance, right here in the palace tonight!' he announced.

The whole kitchen bustled with excitement.

'The king and queen have decided that the royal prince should marry. The ball is for him to choose a wife! We are all invited; every one of us.'

There was a loud cheer and everyone began to prepare for the ball. Food was made, drinks were poured and every person in the palace put on their finest clothes. Only the youngest daughter didn't change. Her outfit was always the same.

'Are you coming to the ball, Tattercoats?' asked the butler.

'No,' answered the youngest daughter, 'I have nothing to wear.'

The butler shrugged his shoulders and went upstairs to help out at the party.

The ball began boldly with trumpets and cheering. The youngest daughter could hear the noise of talking, laughing and dancing above her. Eventually, her curiosity got the better of her and the youngest daughter crept upstairs and peered into the ballroom to see everyone in their finest clothes.

When she saw the prince of the palace she felt her heart pounding. He was so handsome! She had to get a closer look, so she let the coat of weeds fall to the ground and stepped into the ballroom wearing her party dress.

When the prince saw her, he gasped. 'Wow, I've never seen *you* before! Do you want to dance?'

The youngest daughter smiled and they danced the night away.

When the clock struck midnight, twelve chimes rang out. The youngest daughter was having the best time ever but she knew that she was to be up early the next morning to make everyone their breakfast in the palace. She didn't want the prince to know that she was a servant, so she simply said, 'Well, I must go now. Goodbye!'

Then the youngest daughter rushed out of the door, put her coat of weeds back on and went to the kitchen.

The next morning the prince was love struck. He sent out knights on quests to find the youngest daughter but nobody knew who the mysterious girl was. The king and queen could take no more of the prince's constant moaning for her. They decided to hold another ball to see if the mysterious girl would appear again.

Sure enough, as the ball was in full swing, the youngest daughter crept up from the kitchen. She left her coat of weeds outside the ballroom and walked over to the prince. He was delighted! They spent another night dancing and laughing with each other.

But when the twelve chimes rang out, the youngest daughter knew she had to leave. She said farewell and rushed out of the ballroom, collecting her coat of weeds as she went.

The next day, the prince was worse than before. He moaned and wailed. He pined and whined.

'If I don't see that girl again I shall die!' he announced.

So a third ball was held. For a third time the youngest daughter entered the party late after leaving her coat of weeds outside. For a third time she and the prince danced the night away. And for a third time she left the party at midnight.

The prince was worse than ever the next day. He was taken to his bed as he was so ill. He became worse and worse, day by day.

The youngest daughter was in the kitchen preparing lunch for the palace. The butler arrived and said, 'It's no use! We've tried everything!'

'What's wrong?' asked the youngest daughter.

'The prince is on his death bed! If we can't find who this mysterious woman he's been dancing with is, then I'm sure he will die!' he answered.

The youngest daughter gasped and said, 'I'll take the prince some vegetable soup. That will make him feel better!'

'Soup?' cried the butler. 'Soup won't help this!'

'It's worth a try,' smiled the youngest daughter. 'But I must take the soup to him *myself*.'

The butler reluctantly agreed and the youngest daughter set off up the large staircase and into the prince's room. She put a tray with the bowl of soup on top next to his bed and cheerfully said, 'Here you go!'

'I know that voice!' gasped the prince.

He leapt from his bed.

'Is that you under that coat of weeds?' he asked.

The youngest daughter let the coat of weeds fall to the ground.

'It is!' exclaimed the prince. 'I love you! Let's get married!'

'OK!' smiled the youngest daughter.

The wedding preparations were made straight away. The king and queen were delighted to have their son feeling better and thought that the youngest daughter was lovely. Everyone in the land was invited to the wedding party. *Even* the youngest daughter's parents. The youngest daughter asked for her wedding dress to have a long veil over it so that nobody could see her face. She also asked that the food served at the party should contain no herbs and spices.

All was ready.

At the party the wedding guests ate their food, but it wasn't very tasty. It was boring and tasteless. The rich man, his wife, his eldest daughter and his middle daughter chewed the food carefully. Suddenly, the rich man stood up and exclaimed, 'This food is terrible!'

Everyone gasped.

'I now understood what my youngest daughter meant! *Food does love herbs and spices!* What have I done? I threw my youngest daughter out of the house and she loves me best of all!'

Just then, the youngest daughter pulled the veil away from her face.

'Daddy!' she shouted.

'Daughter!' he replied.

They rushed to each other and held one another tightly. Before long the whole family had rushed in for a long over-due group hug. The rich man's family and the royal family became the best of friends. The youngest daughter and the prince were the happiest couple you could imagine and they all lived happily ever after.

Does anybody really live happily ever after? Happiness is usually a temporary emotion. We feel happy when something goes right for us or when someone pays us a compliment. We might think we will be happy when we get a promotion at work or buy a new car. Happiness is sparked by an event or moment that brings a feeling of excitement. But joy is a more long-lasting state of contentment. Joy is the feeling of overall contentment with your circumstances. Perhaps the true ending in a fairy tale should become: 'they lived with joy for the rest of their lives'.

33

The Horse and the Archer

Here we have a folk tale that explores the relationship between a human and an animal. The American Veterinary Medical Association published a paper in 2024 that stated, 'The human-animal bond is a mutually beneficial and dynamic relationship between people and animals that is influenced by behaviours considered essential to the health and wellbeing of both. This bond is beneficial to the mental, physical, and social health of people and animals.' A human–animal bond is not to be underestimated, as we see in this tale.

Once there lived an archer who rode a horse with hooves made of iron. One day, the battle-worn archer was riding his horse when he saw something glowing on the ground. He stopped his horse, slid down from the saddle and realised that it was golden feather. Just as the archer was about to pick up the feather, the horse spoke to him. 'If you touch that feather, you will know the meaning of fear and you will know great sadness.'

'What?' asked the archer. 'Me, scared? Bah! More like if I take the feather to the king, he'll make me rich!'

So, the archer climbed back on to the horse and rode to the king's palace. He then presented the king with the golden feather.

'Archer! You have brought me the feather of the firebird!' said the king. 'But am I not the greatest king in the whole of Russia? Yes, I am. So why bring me only the feather? I want the whole bird … or I'll chop your head off!'

The archer's eyes widened and he ran off to find his horse.

The archer then kneeled at his horse's hooves and told the horse everything.

'I told you not to touch that feather!' boomed the horse. 'But, now is not the time of fear. Go to the king and ask him for one hundred bags of corn.'

The archer went to the king and asked for the hundred bags of corn. Then the archer and the horse threw the corn all over a field outside the palace and hid among the trees. They stayed there until the sun rose. The sun flashed scarlet, and gold. Suddenly, out of the sun flew the firebird. It saw the hundred bags of corn, landed on the ground and began to feast.

The archer and the horse rushed out from the trees. The horse pinned the firebird to the ground with its iron hooves. The archer grabbed and stuffed the bird into a silver cage.

He then presented this to the king, who said, 'Archer, you have brought me the firebird! If you can bring me the firebird, you can bring me anything I want! Go to the edge of the world and bring me back the Princess Vasilisa. She is the most beautiful woman in the world and I want her to be my wife … or I'll chop your head off!'

The archer moaned and ran off to find his horse.

The archer then kneeled at his horse's hooves and told the horse everything.

'I told you not to touch that feather!' boomed the horse. 'But, now is not the time of fear. Go to the king and ask him for a golden tent, fine wine and fine food.'

So, the archer went to the king and asked for the tent, the wine and the food. Then the archer climbed back on to the horse's back and rode for many days and many nights until they came to the edge of the world.

The archer pitched the tent and put the wine and food inside. He and the horse then hid behind a large rock on the beach.

The Princess Vasilisa was rowing a silver boat on the ocean at the edge of the world, and when she saw the golden tent she rowed to the shore. She then climbed out, went into the tent and ate the food. Next, she drank the wine. All of the wine. Eventually she fell fast asleep. The archer then lifted her on to the horse's back and rode as quickly as he could back to the king's palace.

When the king saw the princess he smiled and said, 'Wake her up! She's beautiful!'

When the Princess Vasilisa awoke she said, 'Where am I? What am I doing in this place?'

'Don't be scared!' said the king. 'I am the greatest king in the whole of Russia! And you're going to be my wife.'

'No,' replied Princess Vasilisa. 'No I cannot marry you. Because I said that I would only get married in my wedding dress. And my wedding dress is back at the edge of the world. At the bottom of the ocean and trapped underneath the biggest rock in the world!'

'No problem!' smiled the king. 'Archer! I want you to go to the edge of the world, go to the bottom of the ocean, lift the biggest rock in the world and bring me the Princess Vasilisa's wedding dress … or I'll chop your head off!'

The archer groaned and ran off to find his horse.

The archer then kneeled at his horse's hooves and told the horse everything.

'I told you not to touch that feather!' boomed the horse. 'But, now is not the time of fear. Climb on to my back.'

The archer climbed on to the horse's back and rode for many days and many nights until he came back to the edge of the world. There, the archer and the horse hid behind the same large rock on the beach until they saw a lobster scuttling along the beach. The horse rushed out and pinned the lobster to the sand with his iron hooves.

The lobster squeaked, 'Please don't kill me, I'll do anything!'

'Call your brothers and your sisters from all over the world!' boomed the horse. 'Lift the biggest rock in the world and bring me the Princess Vasilisa's wedding dress.'

'OK!' squeaked the lobster and scuttled off into the sea. Every lobster in the world gathered around the biggest rock in the world and lifted it. The lobster took the wedding dress, scuttled back to the beach and gave it to the horse.

The archer rode as quickly as he could back to the king's palace.

The king smiled and said, 'Now, Princess Vasilisa, will you marry me?'

Princess Vasilisa answered, 'I will only marry you ... IF ... the man who brought that dress is burnt alive in front of my eyes.'

'What?' spluttered the archer.

'No problem,' replied the king. 'Guards, lock the archer up!'

The archer was locked in the dungeon and a huge bonfire was built. When the bonfire was lit and flames were beginning to lick at the sky, the archer was sent for.

The archer begged the king that he might speak to his horse just one last time and the king said, 'Be quick! For I wish to be married!'

The archer then kneeled at his horse's hooves and told the horse everything.

'I told you not to touch that feather!' boomed the horse. 'NOW is the time of fear.'

The archer wailed.

'But … if you jump into the fire yourself. Do not let anyone help you into the fire. Then you will be fine.'

So, the archer was taken to the bonfire. A crowd watched as he took off his robes and pushed back the king's guards. The archer ran forward and leapt into the fire.

After a few moments the archer stepped back out of the fire. As he did, all could see that the archer had changed. He was now young and handsome. The once battle-worn and weary archer was transformed.

'Ooh!' squealed Princess Vasilisa. 'He's *gorgeous*!'

The king heard the princess and said, 'Let me get into the fire! I want to become gorgeous too!'

The king's guards helped him into the fire … but the king did not get back out of the fire again.

Princess Vasilisa quickly became Queen Vasilisa. The archer collected the silver cage from the palace and the firebird was released. It flew straight back into the sun.

'Will you rule with me?' asked Queen Vasilisa.

'I cannot, my queen,' the archer replied, 'I need to be with my family.'

The archer then climbed upon his horse's back and galloped away. He was alone with the only family he ever had and ever wanted.

The horse in this Russian folk tale is the archer's saviour. The horse's words saved the archer's life on more than one occasion. We can learn from animals even when they cannot talk to us. By watching the peaceful sleeping of a cat, we can copy it and try to relax. By looking at a dog's enthusiasm for play, a lion's tenacity or an ant's co-operation to get something done, we might be inspired to mimic these behaviours ourselves. Animals can teach us to take time to rest, live in the now, be patient, work collaboratively and much more.

34

Tchang's Quest

Having friends and family to stay can bring a lot of stress to our lives. However, hospitality can have enormous benefits for us. It helps us build better relationships with people, teaches us empathy and helps us to build a better social network. In this tale, the benefits might be exaggerated, yet perhaps we could all learn to be more hospitable.

Tchang lived with his mother. They lived simple lives and were happy enough, but no matter what they planted, nothing seemed to grow on their farm. One day Tchang said to his mother, 'I'm going to see the Great King of the West, and ask him why nothing grows on our farm.'

Tchang hugged his mother tightly and then set off walking.

He walked for forty-nine days and forty-nine nights, until at last, breathless and panting, he came to a house. He knocked at the door.

An old woman answered and said, 'Why hello there, dear. What can I do for you then?'

Tchang said, 'I'm on my way to see the Great King of the West to ask him a question, but I was just wondering, perhaps I could spend the night here, I'm exhausted.'

The old women smiled a toothless grin and said, 'You're welcome to stay at my place, but would you mind asking the Great King of the West a question for me as well? Would you ask him why my daughter cannot speak?'

Tchang said, 'I shall ask your question.'

He then spent that night sleeping soundly at the house and the next morning he set off walking. He walked for another forty-nine days and forty-nine nights, until at last, breathless and panting, he came to a farm. He knocked at the door.

A farmer answered and said, 'Hello! What can I do for you young man?'

Tchang said, 'I'm on my way to see the Great King of the West to ask him a question, but I was just wondering, perhaps I could spend the night at your place, I'm bone weary.'

The farmer replied, 'Oh you'd be welcome to spend the night here, but could you ask him a question for me as well please? Could you ask him why my fruit trees grow no fruit?'

Tchang said, 'I shall certainly ask your question.'

The next morning, he set off walking. He walked and walked and walked for yet another forty-nine days and yet another forty-nine nights, until at last, breathless and panting, he came to a river. This river was too deep for Tchang to walk across, the currents were too strong for him to swim across and there was no bridge to help him cross over. Tchang thought he was going to have to turn back home, when suddenly the river began to froth wildly. From the white foam there rose a huge and fearsome dragon; a dragon with teeth like razors, eyes like two pools of fire and claws like daggers. The dragon had a pearl in the centre of its forehead that glistened as it roared, 'Who dares to stand on my riverbank?'

Tchang whimpered, 'I need to get to the other side, I'm going to see the Great King of the West to ask him a question.'

The dragon stopped and thought for a moment, then said, 'If I help you to the other side then can you ask the king why I cannot fly as other dragons do?'

Tchang replied, 'I shall ask your question.'

The dragon made itself into a bridge and Tchang walked across to the other side of the river. Tchang then arrived at the Great King of the West's golden palace. It shone like the sun and Tchang was bathed in golden light. He stepped inside and there he saw the Great King of the West, seated upon a golden throne. The Great King of the West stared at Tchang and stroked his long, white beard.

Eventually the king boomed, 'I know why you are here.'

His mighty voice echoed around the glorious, golden room.

'You're here to ask me questions, but know this: you may only ask me *three* questions, no more.'

Tchang thought, 'If I ask the question for the old woman and the farmer *and* the dragon, then I won't be able to ask a question for myself.'

Tchang knew that he had made three promises, so he asked the questions and left.

The dragon was stomping around impatiently on the riverbank.

'Well?' thundered the dragon. 'What did he say?'

Tchang smiled. 'The Great King of the West said that you can't fly like the other dragons because you need to start doing nice things for people. Only then will he grant you your ability to fly.'

The dragon stopped for a moment, thought about this, then plucked the pearl from his forehead and gave it to Tchang. Then the dragon, once again, made himself into a bridge so that Tchang could walk across. Tchang thanked the dragon and began walking. He walked for forty-nine days and forty-nine nights, until at last, breathless and panting, he came to the farm. He knocked at the door.

The farmer answered and said, 'Tchang! You've come back to me! Did you ask my question? Did you ask the Great King of the West why my fruit trees grow no fruit?'

Tchang said, 'Yes I did. The Great King of the West said that we should dig at the roots of each of your nine fruit trees.'

Tchang and the farmer began digging and underneath each of the nine fruit trees were nine boxes. When they unlocked and opened the boxes they saw that each one was filled with golden coins shining in the sunlight. The farmer gave Tchang one of the boxes and wished him luck on his journey. Tchang thanked the farmer and again began to walk.

He walked for the next forty-nine days and forty-nine nights, until at last, breathless and panting, he came to the house of the old woman he met so long ago. He knocked at the door. The old woman answered. 'Tchang! You've come back to me. Thank you so much. Did you ask the Great King of the West my question? Did you ask him why my daughter speaks no words?'

Tchang said, 'Yes I did. Bring your daughter to me.'

The daughter arrived and Tchang knew exactly what to do. He held the dragon's pearl next to her mouth and there was a flash of white light. Suddenly, the daughter could speak. 'Thank you, Tchang!'

Tchang spent the day talking with the girl. That day turned into another. Tchang ended up spending forty-nine days and forty-nine nights at the house. He and the girl had become such close friends that they decided to marry. After they were married, Tchang and his new wife, and his new mother-in-law, walked for another forty-nine days and forty-nine nights until at last, breathless and panting, they came to Tchang's farm. Tchang knocked at the door.

When Tchang's mother answered he saw that she had gone blind because she'd cried so many tears waiting for Tchang to come home. Tchang took the dragon's pearl, held it against her eyes, and this time there were two flashes of white light.

Tchang's mother could then see again!

Tchang then took the dragon's pearl and buried it on the farmland. There was a great, loud rumbling noise and suddenly plants burst forth from the ground. Trees, bushes, groves, shrubberies and many more all came forth bursting with fruit and vegetables. From that day on lots of things grew on Tchang's farm.

The dragon flew back to see Tchang and his family every year and brought many gifts. Tchang, his mother, his wife and his mother-in-law all lived happily ever after.

Kindness might not give us the ability to fly in a literal sense, however figuratively we might feel like we have wings when we help others. According to research, helping others gives you a mental boost by providing you with a neurochemical sense of reward. When you do something kind to help somebody else, your body produces happy hormones and endorphins that foster positive emotions. Focusing on someone else's needs also helps you to forget about your own problems.

35

Monday, Tuesday

Our planet is in crisis. According to the WWF, 'Many of the planet's threatened species live in areas that will be highly affected by climate change. And unfortunately, climate change is developing too quickly for many species to adapt.' This cautionary folk tale tells of an ancient race of beings that knew the benefits of looking after our planet long ago.

There was once a cheerful old man called Lusmore. You could never meet such a nice old man as this one; he always had a kind word and a smile for everybody he met. He had worked hard his whole life and as a result his back was all hunched up on the left side. But this didn't make his mood bad. He was often seen walking up and down the high street hunched up, waving and stopping to ask people how they were.

Now, in this village there lived another old man called Jack Madden. He couldn't have been any more different. This old man was the grumpiest, meanest, rudest old man you could ever meet. He too had worked hard his whole life and as a result was all hunched up on the right side. This made his mood all the worse. He was often seen walking up and down the high street hunched up, grimacing and swearing at everyone he met.

One day, the cheerful old Lusmore was off walking past the high street and decided to go for a small stroll through the woods nearby. He often liked to stop and feed the birds and squirrels in those woods. He stopped, sat down on a fallen tree and was throwing nuts and seeds around when all of a sudden, he heard strange singing coming from the trees beyond.

Singing that went:

'♫ Monday … Tuesday ♫'

then again:

'♫ Monday … Tuesday ♫'

and again:

'♫ Monday … Tuesday ♫'

Lusmore thought that this was the most beautiful singing he had ever heard. He just couldn't help himself; he just had to join in.

When the signing went:

'♫ Monday … Tuesday ♫'

the cheerful old man sang:

'♫ Wednesday … Thursday ♫'

At that moment a whole parade of fairies stepped out from the trees and stood in front of the cheerful old man. Each was no taller than a daffodil and wore sycamore green clothes. They had long, golden hair that shone in the bright sun.

One fairy wearing a golden crown skipped over to the cheerful old Lusmore and spoke. 'Ah, thank you! Thank you so much! We've been singing that song for years and we just couldn't remember the next line. Thank you again. It's a lovely cheerful tune, isn't it?'

'Erm, yes, it is!' beamed Lusmore.

'Is there something you want in return for helping me? Gold perhaps?' asked the fairy king, and as he said this several other fairies pulled up a mighty old box from beneath the ground.

Gold glinted from inside as the fairies opened it.

'Oh, no thank you,' smiled Lusmore. 'Just seeing you happy and enjoying the song is payment enough for me.'

'There must be something I can help you with!' exclaimed the fairy king. 'What about that hunched back on your left side? I can fix that for you!'

'Ah, that would be grand! Thank you!'

With that the fairies all began to sing a different song. A song that went:

'♫ Lusmore! The hunch that you wore is now no more. ♫'
'♫ Look down on the floor to see it, Lusmore! ♫'

Lusmore could not believe it. He stood as straight as a tower and he'd never felt better! His hunch was completely gone from his left side. He cheerfully skipped back home and could hear the fairies singing as he went:

'♫ Monday … Tuesday ♫'
'♫ Wednesday … Thursday ♫'

Lusmore was running up and down the streets of the village and shaking hands with everyone he met. He told his story a hundred times and everyone was overjoyed for the cheerful old man. Everyone, except for the grumpy old Jack Madden.

'You big fool!' he cried out to Lusmore when he heard the story. 'I'd have taken the gold AND got my hunchback fixed too! You great big fool!'

Jack Madden then bought some nuts and seed from the local store and hobbled off into the woods. He immediately started to throw the nuts and the seeds at any animal he saw. Soon enough all of the woodland animals had scattered and were hidden, afraid of being pelted with food.

Then, all was quiet and still in the wood. Jack Madden sat down and listened.

'♫ Monday … Tuesday ♫'
'♫ Wednesday … Thursday ♫'

Jack Madden then called out: 'Friday and Saturday and you forgot about Sunday as well, you little dafties!'

The fairies stepped out from the woods. Their faces were masks of rage. Jack Madden gulped and said, 'Erm, so I helped you with your song, so, erm, can I have some gold then or what?'

The king of the fairies frowned, then snapped his fingers. The other fairies pushed their hands beneath the ground and pulled out the mighty old box. They threw it over to Jack Madden, which nearly knocked him off his feet. But the grumpy old man didn't mind, he grinned as he greedily opened the box and stared at the golden coins inside.

The fairies then turned to walk off into the woods, when Jack Madden called out, 'Hey! Wait on, you little dafties! What about me old hunchback eh? What about fixing that too?'

The fairies flew over and roughly rubbed at Jack Madden's back, then said, 'Get some rest. Then in the morning … you'll see.'

They then fluttered away, disappearing between the trees. Jack Madden then walked off into the woods with a grin on his face singing:

'♫ Monday … Tuesday ♫'
'♫ Wednesday … Thursday ♫'
'♫ Friday … Saturday ♫'
'♫ Sunday … Sunday ♫'

Jack Madden went to bed that night feeling very excited. He put the mighty old box on the floor next to his bed and slipped into peaceful sleep.

His first thoughts in the morning were of his hunch. He pulled himself out of bed and to his horror, discovered that his hunch was still there. And, even worse … now he had one on the left side too! Jack Madden kicked the mighty old box in temper. The lid swung open and there, inside, was no longer golden coins, but instead was dust.

'What?' bellowed Jack Madden. 'I've been tricked!'

He then stomped out of the house and into the woods shouting insults and swearing terribly, searching for the fairies.

As soon as he arrived in the woods, the fairies flew out, disturbed by the grumpy old man's noise. They flew around him and called:

'♫ Jack Madden! Jack Madden! ♫'
'♫ Your words came so bad in. ♫'
'♫ Now your life we will sadden! ♫'
'♫ Away, away goes Jack Madden! ♫'

That grumpy old man was never seen again.

If you go into the woods, and you hear strange singing, then watch out because the fairies reward those who do good and may just punish those who do not.

In this story, the fairies symbolise the environment, reflecting its beauty, balance and generosity. The grumpy man's actions represent human greed and the expectation that nature should endlessly provide for us. Just as he takes from the fairies without giving back, humans have taken from the environment without investing in its wellbeing. The consequences are now clear, as nature, like the fairies, suffers from overuse and neglect. This tale underscores the need to restore balance, showing that taking without gratitude or responsibility leads to inevitable loss.

Looking after our environment has never been more essential. Sir David Attenborough advises, 'Stop waste. Stop waste of any kind. Stop wasting energy, stop wasting food, stop wasting plastic and stop wasting time. This is a precious world and each of us can use our actions and our voice to save our planet.'

36

Jack and the Giant's Daughter

Here we have a third and final tale with Jack as the protagonist.
It features a giant but Jack isn't up to any giant slaying here.
Instead, we have a story of romance. Its triadic structure of tasks
seem impossible but luckily a mysterious and magical daughter
lends a hand ... and a toe.

Once upon a time, there was a young man named Jack who wandered the land in search of adventure. During his travels, he encountered a colossal giant standing between two mountains. Not keen on dealing with giants again, Jack decided to walk in the opposite direction.

'Oi you!' bellowed the giant, his voice echoing through the valley.

Jack, reluctantly turning back, approached the giant and looked up. 'Yeah?'

'Do you want a job?' the giant boomed.

'What kind of job?' Jack asked, curious yet cautious.

'Cleaning my house! It's massive! It'll probably take you ages, let's say a year! If you do a good job, I'll give you a box of golden coins! How does that sound?'

'Alright,' Jack agreed.

Without further ado, the giant scooped Jack up and took him to his home. It was not just a house but a sprawling castle with towering walls, vast courtyards and imposing turrets. Jack immediately set to work, sweeping, scrubbing, polishing and tidying with a vigour he had never known.

As the year drew to a close, Jack surveyed his work with pride. The castle sparkled, except for the tallest tower, which still needed cleaning. Determined to finish, he climbed the winding stairs to the top. In the highest room, he found three daughters of the giant, each more beautiful than the last.

The youngest and most enchanting of the daughters gazed at Jack and said, 'Hello! We've been watching you all year. I think you're very handsome.'

Blushing, Jack stammered, 'Would you like to take a walk with me? Maybe go on a picnic?'

'I'd like that very much,' she smiled, 'but you should ask my father first.'

Jack descended to the courtyard, where the giant was waiting.

'You've done a very good job!' the giant roared approvingly. 'Here's a box of golden coins!'

'Thank you, but I don't want them,' Jack replied, smiling up at the giant.

'What do you mean, you don't want them?'

'I'd like to take your daughter out instead,' Jack said, beaming.

'Do you now?' The giant's eyes narrowed. 'If you want to take my daughter out, you'll have to complete three tasks, each more difficult than the last!'

'No problem!' Jack boasted, feeling confident.

'First, you must clean out my horses' stables! I have seven hundred horses, and the stable hasn't been cleaned for seven years! If you can get it clean by dark, you'll complete the first task. If not, I'll eat you!'

The giant carried Jack to the stables. They were a horrifying sight, with dung piled to the ceiling. Jack began shovelling frantically, but as the day wore on, it seemed like he hadn't made a dent.

Just then, the youngest daughter appeared and asked, 'How are you getting on?'

'Not well at all,' Jack replied, dejected. 'I'm supposed to clean this by sunset, but I'll never manage it.'

'Leave it to me,' she said with a smile.

She stepped into the stable and began to spin on the spot, faster and faster, creating a whirlwind. The dung flew out of the door, forming a neat pile outside.

'There you go!' she said, her eyes twinkling.

'Wow!' Jack exclaimed, genuinely amazed.

'I've left a bit for you to clean up,' she added. 'When my father sees you finishing it, he'll think you did the whole job. See you later!'

As the giant arrived, Jack was just clearing the last bit of dung.

'Well done! You've done very well! But the next task will be even harder!'

That night, Jack slept fitfully, dreading the next challenge. In the morning, the giant arrived and asked, 'Are you ready for task number two?'

Without waiting for an answer, the giant scooped Jack up and carried him to the most northerly part of England.

'This is my holiday cottage!' The giant gestured to a huge, roofless cottage. 'Thatch the roof with birds' feathers! But each feather must come from a different bird! You have until sunset. If you can do it, you've completed the second task. If not, I'll eat you!'

The giant handed Jack a bow and three arrows before leaving. Jack tried to shoot a blackbird but missed. He missed again with a thrush and yet again with a greenfinch. As the day slipped away, he hadn't collected a single feather.

The giant's daughter arrived just then. 'How are you getting on?' she asked.

'Not well,' Jack sighed. 'I'm supposed to thatch that roof with feathers, and I don't have even one!'

'Leave it to me,' she said.

She pulled a slender silver whistle from her dress and blew it. Suddenly, there was a cacophony of squawks as birds from all over the world flew in. Each bird dropped a feather on to the roof, then flew away.

'Place the last feather as my father arrives,' she advised. 'He'll think you did it all.'

Jack inserted the final feather just as the giant returned.

'Well done! You've done very well! But the third task will be the hardest yet!'

That night, Jack slept soundly, confident about the third challenge. In the morning, the giant arrived and boomed, 'Are you ready?'

He picked Jack up and carried him to the most southerly part of England.

'This is the tallest tree in England.' He pointed to a tree whose top disappeared into the clouds. 'At the top, there's a nest with a golden egg. Fetch me that egg before dark, and you can take out my daughter! If not, I'll eat you!'

Jack tried to climb the tree, but the bark was too smooth. He kept slipping and falling. As despair set in, the giant's daughter appeared.

'How are you getting on?' she asked.

'Not well,' Jack admitted. 'Could you fetch the golden egg for me?'

'Sorry, but no,' she replied gently. 'This is something you must do yourself. But I brought something that might help.'

She handed Jack a silver dagger. 'You need to cut my throat and open my chest. Remove my bones and use them as a ladder to climb the tree. After you retrieve the egg, climb down and put my bones back. Pour this potion over me, and I will come back to life.'

Jack stared at her in horror. 'Are you serious? I can't kill you and pull out your bones!'

'You must,' she insisted, placing the dagger in his hand. 'Or my father will eat you.'

With a heavy heart, Jack did as she instructed. He slit her throat, her blood flowing like a crimson river. He sat on her chest and plunged the dagger into her, removing her bones one by one. Stuffing the bones into his pockets and using them as handholds, he climbed the tree.

When he reached the top, he retrieved the golden egg from the nest. On his way down, he collected the bones, but realised too late that he had left one, her little toe, at the top.

'Oops!' Jack muttered to himself. 'I'm sure she won't miss it.'

Back on the ground, he placed the bones back in her body and poured the magic potion over her. The bones reassembled, and her wounds healed instantly.

'Well done, Jack!' she said, standing up and smiling. Then she frowned. 'Hey, where's my little toe?'

'I left it at the top,' Jack admitted sheepishly.

Shaking her head, she muttered to herself and walked away. Just then, the giant arrived.

'Have you got the golden egg?'

'I have,' Jack replied, handing it over.

The giant's face turned crimson with anger. 'Well, I suppose you want to take my daughter out now?' he thundered. 'You can, if you can pick her out!'

He clapped his hands three times, and three identical white swans flew through the air, circling his head. 'One of these is my youngest daughter. If you can identify her, you can take her out.'

Jack scrutinised the swans. He noticed that one of them was missing a toe from its webbed foot.

'That's your youngest daughter,' he said, pointing.

The giant's face grew even redder. He clapped his hands three times. Two swans flew away, and the third landed, transforming back into the giant's daughter.

Jack took her hand, and together they walked away. However, their happiness was short-lived. They argued constantly about one tiny thing … her missing little toe.

In any relationship between a partner, friend or colleague you have to let things go. In order to do this, it can be helpful to pause, think your feelings through and consider other people's perspectives. Empathy is key here. It is how we build social connections and feeling connected to others is hugely important for our optimal wellbeing. It is the very basis of human relationships and helps us to feel valued, loved and cared for.

37

King Solomon and the Djinn

In this tale I have merged several King Solomon stories together from Christianity, Judaism and Islam. In Islam, Solomon is known as Prophet Sulayman. Across all three religions, Solomon is celebrated for his unparalleled wisdom, his role as a just and powerful ruler, and his association with the construction of the Temple in Jerusalem. This story focuses on Solomon's relationship with the djinn, also known as genies.

War raged in Heaven. The djinn, led by their seven kings, had marched upon the realm of paradise in order to overthrow God and the angels and take Heaven for themselves. But God is omniscient and omnipresent. God knew they would come. God had known since the creation of both the djinn and the angels, way before the creation of humans. Angels were made from light and were utterly obedient to God, while the djinn were created from smokeless fire and possessed free will, something that humans would also have upon their creation.

The angels lived in Heaven and the djinn lived in the distant corners of space. The seven djinn kingdoms each had their own king. There was Al Madhhab the golden one, Al Abyad the white, Al Burqan the gleaming, Zawba'ah the green, Al Ahmar the red, Shamhurash the white and Maymun the lucky. It was Al-Madhab who had first sown the seed of discontentment within the djinn.

'Why should the angels live in Heaven while we live in cold darkness? We're more powerful. We have better weapons. We could easily overthrow God and destroy the angels! I will rule Heaven while you live in paradise.'

Al-Madhab sent Iblis to offer his undying adoration to God. Iblis was a very reverent and knowledgeable djinn. He soon won the angels over and was allowed to live in Heaven. Al-Madhab's plan was cunning. He was patient. Only once Iblis had the trust of the angels completely were the seven armies of djinn assembled.

Iblis opened the gates of Heaven and the seven armies of the djinn marched right in. The angels quickly gathered their glowing weapons and armour as the djinn attacked with their flaming swords.

War raged in Heaven for seven years but eventually the angels defeated the rebellious djinn. It was the archangel Michael, known as Mika'il, who overpowered Al-Madhab. The seven kings were killed by Mika'il, then the angel cast Iblis out of Heaven. The rest of the angels then drove the remaining defeated djinn to the far corners of the Earth.

Peace reigned for many years. Then, God decided to create a new being; humans. Adam was the first. He was made from clay. Then came Eve. They lived in earthly paradise but Iblis watched them. He became a serpent and vowed to lead these humans astray as revenge for his downfall. He tempted the humans to eat from the tree of knowledge, then slithered away once they had used their free will to disobey God.

But, with God's guidance, humans prospered and filled the Earth.

After many generations of humans, there came a king named Solomon. This king's wisdom enabled him to teach lessons to all on the transient nature of earthly glory. His devotion to

God was unparalleled and God sent the angel Gabriel, known as Jibreel, to offer Solomon a gift from Heaven.

Jibreel appeared before Solomon in a dream and offered the king anything he wanted. Solomon asked only for God's love and nothing more. Jibreel further offered riches beyond the king's wildest dreams but Solomon refused these, saying that all he wanted was God's love.

When Solomon awoke from his dream two gifts had been left in his bed chamber. The divine messenger had given Solomon a huge, green flying carpet and a ring that bore God's name upon it. This ring gave Solomon the power to command all living things upon the Earth. He was now the king of all of Earth.

Solomon flew on his huge carpet over the whole world. On these travels he noticed the djinn. They were causing mayhem and mischief all across the Earth, tempting humans into diso-beying God. So, Solomon used his ring and commanded each of the djinn to be trapped inside of lamps, bottles, jars and other vessels. He then flew all around the world and cast each vessel into the sea.

Solomon ruled wisely for forty years before his death. He was then buried in the city of David, his father, and his son Rehoboam reigned after him.

As for the djinn, the ring and the king that had commanded them to enter their vessels meant that they could not escape by themselves. The Seal of Solomon held them in their pris-ons. So instead, the djinn had to persuade humans to release them. They did this by offering the humans three wishes in return for their release.

But the djinn were crafty and manipulative. Their wishes were often the promise of riches, or power but these often led to the person's ruin.

Once the djinn were released they joined Iblis, who had created his own kingdom of hell. There Iblis had given himself a new name. He called himself Shaytan, ruler of hell. The djinn joined their new king and continued to tempt humans to disobey God by appealing to human desires, pride and weaknesses. From their new home, the djinn spread doubt and deception in order to distance people from their faith. However, through faith, prayer and righteous living the djinn would always be powerless.

In the Book of Ecclesiastes from the Old Testament of the Hebrew Bible, King Solomon says that we only have one life on Earth and we never know how long this life will be, therefore we should live each day as if it were our last. When we do this, we become more aware of the preciousness of life. This mindset helps us appreciate the small moments, the beauty around us and the people in our lives, thus fostering a deeper sense of gratitude.

38

The Soldier and Death

Our mortality may be a subject that we ponder often or perhaps never. According to the 2017 'Survey of American Fears' conducted by Chapman University, 20.3 per cent of Americans are 'afraid' or 'very afraid' of dying. Death is an inevitability, but should we fear it? The Stoic philosopher Epicurus said, 'Why should I fear death? If I am, death is not. Why should I fear that which cannot exist if I do?' These are words to ponder upon. In the meantime, here we have a folk tale that explores what a world would look like if there was no death.

A soldier was walking along a dusty road. He was returning home to his wife and son after a long battle and was weary to the bone. Along the road he saw an old man who was sat on the ground with a deck of cards in front of him. The old man smiled a toothless, genuine smile.

He then lifted up the cards and performed the most amazing card tricks the soldier had ever seen. The old man then encouraged the soldier to pick cards and memorise them. The old man guessed correctly every card that the soldier had put back in the deck, even after shuffling faster than his eyeballs could move.

'You're amazing!' the soldier beamed.

'Worth a coin?' the old man asked.

'Much more! But I have nothing. Nothing but a couple of dried biscuits in my pocket. You can have one of those if you like!'

He handed the old man a biscuit and smiled again.

'You seem like a good man,' the old man sighed. 'Here, take my cards. Play any game with those and you will be the winner.'

'I can't take those!' the soldier said with a furrowed brow.

But the old man insisted so much that the soldier found himself walking along the road once more with a magical deck of hands in his pocket.

After a while, he saw an old woman sat on the side of the road. She had a sack and she too was performing the most astonishing magic tricks. She pulled out handkerchiefs, flowers and even rabbits, one after the other.

'You're amazing!' the soldier beamed.

'Worth a coin?' she asked.

'Much more! But I have nothing. Nothing but a dried biscuit in my pocket. You can have half of that if you like!'

He snapped the biscuit in two, but as he was handing it over to the old woman, it didn't feel right giving her half, so he handed over the lot. The old woman smiled.

'You seem like a good man,' the old woman sighed. 'Here, take my sack. Anything you order into that sack will have to get into it in a flash!'

'I can't take that!' the soldier laughed.

But the old woman insisted so much that he found himself walking along the road again with a magical deck of cards in one pocket and a magical sack in the other.

A lake was just ahead of him, so he strolled over and saw a flock of geese paddling across the surface.

'Oi! Geese!' he shouted.

The geese turned to look at what was making the noise.

'You see this sack? Get in it!'

All nine geese raced over with a great flapping and honking. They zoomed into the sack and nearly knocked the soldier off his feet.

He smiled, flung the sack on to his back and whistled a merry tune as he walked to the nearest inn.

'Landlord!' he grinned. 'I have nine geese in this sack. If you cook one for me and give me a bed for the night then the other eight are yours!'

The landlord was delighted. As was the soldier who ate, drank and slept so well that in the morning he felt better than he had in years.

When he opened the curtains of his bedroom, he saw a king's palace in the distance on top of a hill above the town. But this once magnificent palace was no longer splendid: the roof tiles were broken or missing, the windows were shattered or smashed, the walls were crumbling or cracked.

The soldier walked downstairs, collected his sack and asked the landlord why such a beautiful palace was left in such ruin.

'Oh, these are terrible times,' the landlord grumbled. 'The king, queen and all of their servants have fled the palace. Demons live there now! Demons that play their card games all night and get up to all kinds of mischief.'

'Card games you say?' the soldier smiled.

So off he went, walking towards the palace with his magical deck of cards in one pocket and his magical sack in the other.

He then sat in the throne room playing with the cards and waited.

Night fell like lead, filling the gloomy palace with head-stone greys and spider soul blacks. The soldier lit a candle and whistled a merry tune.

As the clock struck midnight there was a gust of wind and the candle was snuffed out.

The soldier relit it and saw a legion of demons before him.

'Hello!' they screeched.

'Hello there!' the soldier smiled.

'What have we got here then?' one of the demons leered.

'An old man!' another croaked.

'An old man that wants to die!' laughed another.

'Old men can be a bit chewy, but we'll give it a go!'

They laughed and jeered but the soldier kept smiling as he produced his deck of cards.

'Fancy a game?' he asked.

They couldn't resist! They agreed to play poker, a demon's game, the stakes were high: if the soldier won, he got gold, if the demons won, they got him! But winning was something that came easy when you had a deck of magical cards. The soldier won hand after hand, game after game. The demons became beyond infuriated. They pulled their own ears and horns, they slammed their claws on to the table and the soldier just kept winning. When they had no more gold to offer the soldier stood up.

'Well, thank you for a lovely evening!' the soldier said, putting the cards in his pocket.

'What's to stop us tearing you apart anyway!' the demons screeched.

'This!' the soldier replied and slammed his magical sack on to the table.

'What's that?' one demon asked.

'A sack!' answered another.

'Is that meant to scare us?' another laughed.

'You see this sack?' asked the soldier, opening the sack wide open. 'Get in it!'

The whole legion of demons flew over to the sack with a great roaring and gnashing. They whooshed into the sack in a flash.

The soldier smiled, flung the sack on to his back and whistled a merry tune as he walked out of the palace. He then slammed the sack on to the floor and began jumping up and down on top of it.

The demons wailed.

He kicked the sack right the way round the whole palace.

The demons howled.

He threw the sack here there and all over.

The demons begged for mercy.

He opened the sack just a fraction.

'Will you leave this place and promise never to return?' he asked.

'We promise!' the demons wailed.

The soldier opened the sack and the demons shot out, racing to Hell. But as the last demon flew out, the soldier grabbed its hoof-foot.

'Not you! You will be my servant! Agreed?'

'Agreed! Just let me go!' the demon screeched.

'I'll take this to remind you who you belong to!'

The soldier ripped off its foot and let the sobbing demon fly away. Stuffing the foot into his pocket, he walked back towards the town below whistling a merry tune.

News soon spread that the soldier had rid the palace of the fearsome demons. The king and queen were delighted. They moved right back in. The moved their servants in. They even moved the soldier in!

He soon became the king's best friend and his most trusted advisor. He sent for his wife and son, and all three of them lived together again in the splendour of the palace.

But on the son's tenth birthday, he became very ill.

Doctors and physicians were sent for but none of them could make him well. Days passed and the boy got worse.

The soldier remembered his demon and pulled out the hoof-foot from his pocket, then demanded that it should appear.

There was a puff of green smoke.

'Hello!' the demon screeched. 'Ooh, you look like you've done well for yourself!'

'Indeed I have, but I need your help!'

The demon looked at the poorly boy. The demon then pulled out a glass that was tucked into his belt. The glass was filled with water and the demon peered through the water at the boy once more.

'Look through this!' the demon said. 'You see that black-cloaked figure standing at the feet of your boy? That is Death. It is good that Death is at your boy's feet. If Death was at his head, then I would be able to do nothing!'

'Can you cure him?' asked the soldier. 'If you do then I'll give you your foot back!'

The demon flashed a toothy grin, dipped its claws into the water and flicked this water at the boy.

The boy sat up.

The boy got up.

The boy was better!

'Thank you!' beamed the soldier. 'Here's your foot. I'll tell you what, give that glass to me and I'll give you your freedom!'

'Deal!' squealed the delighted demon.

In a puff of green smoke, he was gone.

So, off the soldier went in search of more adventure with his magical deck of cards in one pocket, his magical sack in the other and his magical glass of water in his hands.

He travelled the land curing the sick and needy. For money, of course.

He healed people all over the country. He also cured cats, he mended mice, he healed hounds. He was famous.

But then he was summoned back to the palace. The king was sick. The king was dying.

The soldier got there as quickly as he could, but when he looked through his magic glass, he saw Death at the king's head.

The soldier shook his head.

'You wander this land curing people and pets but you won't cure your king?!' shouted the queen. 'What kind of friend are you?'

The soldier rubbed his chin and thought.

He looked through the glass at Death.

'Death, can you hear me?'

Death nodded once.

'Death, will you take me in the king's place?'

Death nodded once.

The king sat up.

The king got up.

The king was better!

But the soldier felt terrible. He was taken to his bed. He looked through the glass and saw Death standing at his head.

'Death, can you hear me?'

Death nodded once.

'Death, do you see this sack?'

Death nodded once.

'Get in it!'

Death flew into the sack. The soldier closed it up and leapt from his bed.

'I've caught Death!' he shouted. He ran around the palace shouting, 'I've caught Death! I've caught Death! I've caught Death!' Over and over again.

He ran into the town and told everyone. Now he was even more famous. He was the soldier that had captured Death. There would be no more death in this world, not for anyone!

So, people got older and older, but no one died.

Wars were fought, but no one died.

People got sick, but no one died.

The soldier was delighted.

After many years, the soldier was a very, very old man, but not as old as the army of aged people that marched upon the palace, begging to die. They had lived long enough. They wanted to be with their loved ones in Heaven.

The soldier nodded. He understood. He knew what he had to do. He had hidden Death by hanging the sack from the tallest tree that sat upon the biggest mountain.

The soldier climbed both the mountain and the tree, then brought the sack down.

He opened the sack wide.

'You can go now, Death!'

Death shrieked in terror and flew away.

Death had returned to this world.

As the years passed, the soldier's wife was taken by Death.

His son was taken by Death.

But the soldier was not.

Death was now scared of him. Death would never come for him.

The soldier eventually became a very, very, very old man. He too wanted to die. He wanted to see his wife and son. He wanted to see his friends and his family.

So off he went in search of a final adventure with his magical deck of cards in one pocket, his magical sack in the other, his magical glass of water in his hands and an idea in his head.

He walked and he walked and he walked. All the way to end of the Earth.

All the way to Hell.

The soldier hammered at the gates of Hell.

A demon opened the gates and peered at him.

'Do you remember me?' the soldier asked.

The demon nodded quickly.

'Do you remember my sack?'

The demon glanced at the sack, then back at the soldier and nodded.

'I want ten thousand souls released from Hell … now!'

'Not a chance!' screeched the demon.

The soldier pulled out the sack.

'Five thousand!' it shouted with a voice full of fear.

The soldier opened the sack.

'Oh, all right then.'

The demon went off mumbling to itself.

The gates were opened wide and ten thousand people all spilt out of Hell.

The soldier led them all the way to the other end of the Earth. All the way to Heaven.

As they all arrived at the pearly gates they were met by St Peter.

'Hello!' smiled the soldier. 'I've brought you ten thousand souls from Hell. Can we come in please?'

'The souls may enter,' replied St Peter, 'but you may not.'

'Oh,' the soldier said.

The ten thousand began marching into Heaven.

The soldier grabbed hold of one of the people at the back and said, 'Take this sack with you. When you get inside, order me into the sack and I'll be with you quick as a flash!'

The soldier sat down and waited.

And waited.

And waited more.

But he was never ordered into that sack.

So, he returned to his wandering. Not welcome in Hell. Not welcome in Heaven. Never being taken by Death.

Still wandering the Earth to this day.

This folk tale from Russia explores a world that has no death in it. We see the necessity of death here and how the soldier longs for his life to end. The Stoic philosopher Marcus Aurelius stated in Meditations, *'It is not death that a man should fear, but he should fear never beginning to live.' So, let's embrace today and celebrate that we are alive.*

Bibliography

Bettelheim, B., *The Uses of Enchantment: The Meaning and Importance of Fairy Tales* (Penguin, 1991)

Carruthers, A., *Cinderella and Other Girls Who Lost Their Slippers* (Pook Press, 2015)

Chiba, K., *Tales of Japan* (Chronicle Books, 2019)

Fry, S., *Heroes* (Penguin, 2019)

Fry, S., *Mythos* (Penguin, 2017)

Grimm, J. and Grimm, W., *The Complete First Edition of the Original Folk and Fairy Tales of the Brothers Grimm* (Princeton University Press, 2014)

Lunge-Larson, L., *The Troll with no Heart in His Body and Other Tales of Trolls from Norway* (Houghton Mifflin, 1999)

Nhat Hanh, T., *The Dragon Prince: Stories and Legends from Vietnam* (Parallax Press, 2007)

Pechackova, I., *The Legend of the Golem* (Meander, 2000)

Reader's Digest, *Folklore, Myths and Legends of Britain* (Reader's Digest, 1977)

Shelton, A., *Tibetan Folk Tales* (Evinity, 1925)

Sherlock, P., *Anansi the Spider Man: Jamaican Folk Tales* (Macmillan, 1959)

Storr, W., *The Science of Storytelling* (William Collins Books, 2019)

Westwood, J. and Simpson J., *The Lore of the Land, A Guide to England's Legends* (Penguin Reference, 2005)

Wong, E., *Tales of the Dancing Dragon: Stories of the Tao* (Shambhala Publications, 2007)